The Adventures of Tassel the Elf

by D. L. Lawrence

Illustrated by Rhiannon Thomas

Incantus Media

First edition published 2014 by Incantus Media
Copyright © Incantus Media
Illustrations © Rhiannon Thomas

ISBN: 978-0-9928016-2-5

Introduction

WALES. The land of song, sorcery, myth, magic and mystery. The land of druids and legends. It was once the home of Merlin, who many claimed to be a wizard. In this land anything is possible.
I have lived here all my life.
I have seen and heard of many strange and unexplainable things.
The stories between these pages are magical and unexplainable.

D.L.Lawrence

The Adventures of Tassel the Elf

By

D. L. Lawrence.

1. The Black Crystal

It was a warm summer morning and Tassel, the little elf who lived in a little cottage with a garden that reached to the Sparkling Silver Stream, had awakened early. He had left the little cottage, walked through the beautiful garden and was standing on the grassy bank looking into the Sparkling Silver Stream. He was dressed in a blue shirt and trousers, with a red hat and matching boots. Around his waist was a silver belt.

Tassel often sat on the grassy bank and watched the sparkling water as it made its way to the sea. This morning felt different. Today something was calling him. He looked at his little boat that he had built himself. He had painted it brown, and it had a white sail. He untied it and made it ready to sail. Then he set off upstream. This morning was certainly different.

A little way upstream lived two of Tassel's very good friends: Sparkle, the fairy of the Sparkling Silver Stream, and Michael, the leprechaun. Sparkle lived in an underwater Magical Cave. Michael lived in the Green Woodland, nobody knew exactly where, for leprechauns liked to have secrets.

It had taken most of the morning before Tassel was approaching Sparkle's underwater Magical Cave. He didn't have to call his friends as they were standing on the grassy bank watching him sailing towards them. Michael was dressed in emerald green with a brown belt and matching brown boots. The brown belt at his waist had a gold buckle. Sparkle was dressed in a light blue gown with a white ribbon at her waist. Her long golden hair flowed around her shoulders. Michael greeted Tassel, 'Good morning, Tassel! You must have started out early this morning.'

'Yes,' replied Tassel, 'something is calling me and I don't know what it is, or why.'

'Yes, I sensed it too, but it wasn't calling me,' said Michael.

3

'I will leave my boat here,' said Tassel as he tied it to some reeds.

'Would you like us to come with you?' asked Sparkle.

'No, thank you. I don't think it's anything bad. It is over this way.' Tassel was pointing in the direction of the little Woodland Cottage. 'I will see you on my way back,' he said.

Tassel waved goodbye and walked on purposefully into the Green Woodland. He passed the little Woodland Cottage but he was still being called on. It wasn't long before he found himself entering the Great Meadow. He was greeted by two or three wood nymphs. They all looked the same, dressed in light green with brown hair.

'This way!' they said.

They chattered amongst themselves, and Tassel could only understand a little of their chatter, words like 'Sparkling Silver Stream,' and 'He is a friend of the leprechaun, you know,' and 'The fairy of the Sparkling Silver Stream,' and 'He lives in a little cottage further downstream'.

Then Tassel could suddenly understand all they said.

'Tassel, you have arrived,' one of the wood nymphs said.

'Arrived where?' asked Tassel.

'Go! He is waiting for you,' persisted the wood nymph.

'Who is?' asked Tassel.

He looked around him, but the wood nymphs had gone. Then he heard a voice. 'Thank you for coming,' it said.

Tassel turned to see the Great Wizard. He had light brown hair, and he wore a black cloak fastened with a golden leaf clasp. It had flashes of gold in it, and it was folded around him. His golden-coloured eyes matched the gold in his cloak. Under his cloak his clothes were a dark purple, and on his feet he wore brown boots.

'I heard something calling me,' said Tassel.

'I called you,' said the Great Wizard. 'I know you, and your two friends look after the Green Woodland and the Sparkling Silver

Stream. But something is coming and it will spread darkness all around. There is a Black Crystal, so dense and filled with darkness that my words could not describe it. It has come from the deepest depths of the Earth, and it will emerge at the far side of the Green Woodland into the Sparkling Silver Stream.'

'How can I stop it?' asked Tassel.

'You can't,' answered the Great Wizard.

Tassel looked at the Great Wizard. 'Can you stop it?' he asked.

'No,' came the reply. 'Where darkness is, light will follow, but I fear not for some time. It will change the Great Meadow and the Green Woodland. It will even change the Sparkling Silver Stream.'

'What can I do?' asked Tassel.

'Help your friends and others that will need your help during this dark time,' said the Great Wizard. 'Show hope to all the little people in the Green Woodland and beyond, to the sea.'

'I have not been to the sea,' stated Tassel.

'Just follow the Sparkling Silver Stream. I will watch and help you where and when I can. Go back to your friends and tell them what I have told you. Tassel, you are about to start the biggest, most dangerous adventure of your life.'

Tassel looked across the Great Meadow and then turned to face the Great Wizard, but he had vanished. Two or three little wood nymphs appeared in front of him.

'This way,' they said. Tassel followed them across the Great Meadow and then they vanished. Even now, as Tassel was walking back to his friends, the Black Crystal was emerging from the Earth and entering the Sparkling Silver Stream.

The Sparkling Silver Stream slowly lost its sparkle. The Black Crystal was pushed along the bed of the Silver Stream by the water. It rolled through many underwater passageways, until at last it came to rest under the little Woodland Cottage where a grey-haired old lady lived, and then, it started to change things.

One dark night, the Woodland Cottage became the Black Castle, and the grey-haired old lady became the Black Witch. At the same time, the Great Meadow became a maze, a place not to venture into alone.

When the Great Wizard saw this, he made all the wood nymphs invisible. They would stay this way until this dark time had passed.

While all this was happening, there was another that the darkness was affecting. This was the Goblin King. He was big and round, dressed in brown shirt and trousers. He wore a big black belt with a black buckle. His boots were also very big, and black as night. Most of his goblin band was of the same appearance.

He lived with his band of goblins in the goblin caves, at the far side of the Great Meadow, which had now become a maze. He was not a nice goblin, for it would be difficult to find a nice goblin. The Goblin King lead the band of goblins, and the darkness that was finding its way into everything was making him much worse than he would be. The darkness spread through everything; the Silver Stream no longer sparkled and the Green Woodland slowly changed into the Black Forest.

2.The Luminous Elf

Far away, but not far from the place where the land meets the sea, there is a little cottage with a big garden and a Silver Stream at the bottom of it. This was no ordinary cottage, or garden, for in it lived an elf named Tassel.

He would play in the garden all day in the sunshine. At night he would creep into the cottage and help himself to the food in the kitchen. He was a very happy little fellow, dressed in blue with a silver belt, red hat and red boots.

The attic was the warmest place in the cottage and this is where he spent his winter nights. He would spend hours talking to the spiders that lived in the attic, as he watched them spinning their webs over and around the old oak beams that made up the roof of the cottage.

There was a man and woman who lived in the cottage with their two children, a little boy and a little girl. Though Tassel liked the children very much, he never allowed them to see him. When it was time for the children to go to bed he would creep into their bedroom and listen to their Mother as she told them stories of gnomes and elves like himself. He never did discover how she knew about the little people, unless she had seen him once upon a time, when she was a little girl.

Tassel had a very pleasant, easy life at the cottage until one midsummer night. The moon was full, its light covered everything in the garden and Tassel was walking along the garden path to the cottage. When he reached the shadows of the back door to his amazement he was glowing. The moonlight had stuck to him and he was shining as brightly as a candle flame. Though he looked very pretty it was a terrible thing, for it meant everyone could see him. Before, he had the power to become invisible with just the wave of his hand, as most elves could, but not now. The dust in the moonlight had made him luminous. He didn't know what to do. He couldn't stay outside, so he slipped quietly into the cottage and made his way to the children's bedroom. Their mother was telling them a story about fairy circles and magic wishes.

After a while the children went to sleep, and as the woman knew such a lot about the little people, Tassel decided to ask her advice.

She had tucked her children into their warm beds and was about to leave the bedroom when Tassel spoke to her.

'Excuse me, just a minute, over here!' he called.

He had been sitting on a cotton reel in the corner of the room. When the woman turned and saw him he stood up.

'I am an elf and my name is Tassel.'

'Shhh!' the woman said, 'You will wake the children.'

'I am in terrible trouble,' whispered Tassel, 'will you help me?'

The woman tip-toed across the room and knelt down next to the elf. 'Of course I will, if I can,' she said softly.

Tassel told her how the moonlight had stuck to him and made him luminous. Then he sat down on the cotton reel and listened to the woman, as she told him all she knew about the moonlight.

'The only place I know that glows as brightly as the moon is the sea,' she whispered.

Tassel listened intently and the woman went on. 'Somehow it reflects the moonlight and becomes luminous, just like you. I don't know how to help you, but I think you will find the answer at the seaside. Just follow the stream at the bottom of the garden. It isn't far. All the water goes eventually to the sea.'

'Thank you,' said Tassel as he walked to the bedroom door, 'I will go to the sea, and if I ever return to this little cottage I will grant you three wishes.'

He waved his hand in the air as he often did when he wanted to disappear, but this time he didn't because of the moonlight that was stuck to him. The woman thought he was waving goodbye to her and so she waved back. Tassel shrugged his shoulders, turned and stepped through the open door, leaving the woman still kneeling on the floor, wondering if she had really seen the little elf.

It didn't take Tassel long to reach the Silver Stream. He untied his little boat, the one that he had built himself. It was brown with a white sail. He often used it for going to visit his two very good friends Michael, the leprechaun, and Sparkle, the fairy of the Silver Stream. Sometimes he would use it to go on picnics to the other side of the Silver Stream, but tonight he set off to the sea. He hoisted the white sail and a gentle breeze sent him on his way. He had never been to the sea before and it would be a very long voyage for him.

The moon was still shining brightly so he could see everything quite clearly. He steered his little boat quite expertly between the reeds and big stones that lay in his path.

Once or twice a big eel came to look at the little craft, brushing it with its tail and nearly throwing Tassel into the water.

Tassel shouted to the eel to stay clear of his boat as he was going to the sea. The eel muttered something that Tassel didn't quite hear and then dived into the depths of the Silver Stream.

Tassel had been travelling all night, and as the sun was just rising over the horizon, making tiny droplets of dew sparkle on the grassy banks of the Silver Stream, a big green frog called to him as he sailed by.

'That boat isn't big enough to sail into the big pond,' he croaked.

'Where is the big pond?' asked Tassel.

'It's just around the next bend. It's very salty and we never go there.'

'Never go there,' repeated another voice just in front of the little boat.

Tassel steered to his right and just managed to avoid the head of a large newt.

'It's dangerous in the big pond,' said the newt.

Tassel's little boat was now out of control and, though both the frog and the newt tried to help, the little boat crashed into the bank of the Silver Stream and became stuck fast in the sand.

Tassel was lying flat on his back in the bottom of the boat, his feet kicking in the air, when he heard a voice.

'Good morning, the Fairy Sea Queen is expecting you.'

Tassel staggered to his feet and climbed on to the bank of the Silver Stream to be confronted by a sea sprite. He was dressed in blue from his head to his feet, and was a little bit bigger than Tassel. He had gold-coloured eyes. Tassel thought this a bit strange as he had not seen any other fairy folk with gold-coloured eyes.

'My name is Surf. Follow me, please. The Fairy Sea Queen's cave is over here.'

'How did you know I was coming?' asked Tassel.

'Not all the moondust fell on the sea last night and it only falls on magical people. You are the only elf living close to the Silver Stream and so we knew you would bring the moondust where it belongs.'

The sea sprite stood back from Tassel and looked at him.

'You do shine brightly, don't you?' he said, with a smile.

'It's very irritating, shining like this,' said Tassel. Then he asked a question. 'Have you ever seen the Fairy Queen?'

'No,' answered Surf, 'but others have. They say she is like an old witch dressed in black with white hair and wrinkled skin.'

The two little people walked across the sandy beach to the

entrance of a big, dark cave.

'In you go,' said Surf, 'she is waiting in there for you.'

Now Tassel had had many adventures, but this looked as though it might be the most frightening. He ventured slowly into the darkness of the cave, shining like a little lantern. The passage seemed to go on and on, but at last he arrived in a big cavern with a big rock pool that shone as brightly as he did. At the side of the pool there was a figure, dressed in black with white hair and a wrinkled face, it was the Fairy Sea Queen.

'Please come in, Tassel,' she said.

Tassel walked boldly over to her and said, 'I thought Fairy Queens were beautiful.'

'I was once,' said the Fairy Sea Queen as she took a silver wand from under her black cloak. 'It's the salt in the sea water, it gets into my hair and wrinkles my skin.'

'Why don't you magic it away?' asked Tassel.

'Do you ever use your magic powers for yourself?' she asked.

'Certainly not,' replied the elf.

'Then your question is answered,' said the Fairy Sea Queen.

She touched Tassel's little red hat, that was perched on his head, with the silver wand. The luminous moondust fell from the little elf like snow, and lay in a neat mound around his feet.

'It's dust,' said Tassel. 'I thought it was moonlight.'

The Fairy Sea Queen quickly brushed the moondust into a small glass jar and then empted it into the rock pool.

'Is the pool very deep?' asked Tassel.

'Yes, very deep,' replied the Fairy Sea Queen. 'Thank you for bringing the moondust where it belongs, you may go home now, all your magic powers are restored.'

Tassel waved his hand as he had done many times before and vanished. A few moments passed and he appeared again.

'Fairy Queen,' he said, 'thank you for freeing me from the

luminous moondust.'

She smiled, 'Goodbye Tassel, and it's Fairy Sea Queen,' she corrected him.

Tassel stood quite still, summoning all the magic he possessed, and pointed at the Fairy Sea Queen. A bright blue flash shot from his fingers and engulfed the Fairy Sea Queen in brilliant blue light. Slowly the light faded and the cavern was in darkness except for the rock pool that still shone with moondust.

'Now you are a beautiful, Fairy Sea Queen,' said Tassel. 'The salt from the sea water won't affect you ever again.'

The Fairy Sea Queen looked at her reflection in the rock pool. Her eyes were a deep luminous green, her hair was golden. Her black cloak had been changed into velvet blue, and around her waist was a brown belt with a gold buckle. Her blouse was dark green, as was her dress, and a brown waistcoat had appeared, with yellow laces. Her face and hands had lost the hardness that the sea salt had created. She was beautiful.

'Thank you, Tassel,' she said.

'It's my privilege, your Majesty,' said Tassel, taking off his little red hat and bowing graciously. 'I must go now, your Highness, I have made a promise to a lady and I must keep it.'

'Of course you must,' said the Fairy Sea Queen. She watched as the little elf left her cave.

'Tassel,' she called after him, 'you are always welcome.'

'Thank you, your Majesty,' he called back and then he vanished from her sight.

It was mid morning when he stepped out onto the sandy beach, and Surf was waiting for him.

'Well, what is she like? Is she wrinkled and ugly?' he asked.

Tassel answered firmly. 'She is a Fairy Sea Queen and has more magical power than you or me.'

The sea sprite said no more on the subject as they crossed the sandy beach and eventually reached the Silver Stream. To Tassel's surprise he found his boat had been pulled out of the sand and was tied to a reed waiting for him.

The frog and the newt were nearby smiling at him.

'Did you pull my boat out of the sand?' he asked.

'It was the least we could do,' said the frog.

'We could do,' repeated the newt.

'It wouldn't have been stuck in the sand if it hadn't been for that stupid newt,' added the frog.

'Stupid newt,' repeated the newt.

Surf, the frog and the newt began to laugh.

'It is very nice here. You have all been very good to me. Perhaps I will come and see you again,' said Tassel.

As he boarded his little brown boat his ears were filled with cries from his new friends.

'Come and see us again.'

'Don't wait too long.'

'Good luck on your journey home.'

So Tassel started his voyage home to grant three wishes to a lady who had helped him, but that's another story.

3.The Rainbow Makers

Chapter One - The Storm

'I think it should go from one side of the sky to the other.'

'I think it should go from the middle to the ground.'

'I think it should…'

'Well, I don't.'

The two little elves had been arguing for days. Their names were Evergreen and Pinefloat, and they were identical. They dressed the same, talked the same, they looked the same in every way. But they never could agree on any thing.

Today they were dressed in red suits, with brown boots. Around their waists they both had brown belts with silver buckles. On their heads they wore identical hats.

The little elves had been everywhere and seen everything together. While on their travels they had collected the most beautiful colours they could find, and put them in an old treasure chest. They were now arguing how, and where, to make a Rainbow. But they could not agree on where it should go. It had never been done before and so it was quite a task, as they didn't know what it should look like. However, one thing was decided and that was that the Rainbow would appear in the sky after a storm. The beautiful colours would cheer everyone up and brighten up a grey sky.

A few more days passed and eventually Evergreen and Pinefloat agreed. The Rainbow would be placed in the sky and would start at the highest point. It would flow to the horizon and where it touched the ground a pot of gold would be buried.

Evergreen and Pinefloat had become quite bored since they had stopped arguing, and so it was with smiling faces that they greeted the grey afternoon sky, and the raindrops. They watched eagerly as the raindrops became bigger and bigger. It wasn't long before lightning filled the sky and the sound of thunder rolled around the clouds.

The two little elves could hardly wait for the storm to stop, so that they could start to make their Rainbow. They had already opened their treasure chest and were placing the colours, which were in the shape of little gems, inside a magic bubble that Evergreen had made. When they had finished, they were so eager to send the magic bubble into the sky that they didn't wait for the storm to end.

Evergreen picked up the bubble (which was almost as big as himself) and gently pushed it into the air. The two elves watched as the bubble floated into the sky, they watched until it was a tiny dot. Then it burst. The most beautiful colours in the world floated across the sky like ribbons.

Now it was Pinefloat's turn. He had made a magic bubble and had taken a pot of gold from their treasure chest. He waved to Evergreen and stepped inside his bubble.

'I will see you at the end of the Rainbow,' he said.
Evergreen gave the bubble a push and watched as his friend floated up to the top of the Rainbow.

It wasn't long before Pinefloat stepped out of his bubble on to the Rainbow, which now stretched all the way down to the ground. Pinefloat held his pot of gold tightly and popped his bubble with his finger.

'Oh, I am going to enjoy this,' he said to himself as he took a little run to the slope of the Rainbow, and then sat down, his pot of gold on his lap. He was using the Rainbow as a giant slide and where he came down was where he would bury the pot of gold. It was still raining and Pinefloat was beginning to get wet. The sound of thunder still echoed around the grey clouds as he slid on his way down the coloured ribbons of light.

Pinefloat could see it coming and so could Evergreen, though he was far below on the ground. A long streak of light was heading straight for Pinefloat. There was no time to use any magic. The long streak of pointed light was lightning, and suddenly it hit the Rainbow just in front of Pinefloat.

Colours flew in all directions. The whole sky was alight with colour. Pinefloat found himself falling, tumbling helplessly down, his pot of gold gone. He only hoped that he would land somewhere soft.

Evergreen watched for a long time, until all the colours were gone and the sky was grey again. He wandered in the rain calling his friend but there was no reply. He walked on until he was very tired and wet, and then he sat down under a big tree and began to cry.

Chapter Two - Red

Evergreen and Pinefloat were not the only ones to see the beautiful colours in the sky. Most of the animals and all of the fairy folk that lived in the Black Forest had seen them. One such little fellow was Michael. He was a leprechaun and he had lived in the Black Forest for a very long time. He had a beaming face and always wore a smile, well almost always. He was dressed in a suit of emerald green, with brown boots and at his waist was a brown belt, with a gold buckle. He was a happy fellow but never as happy as when he was with his friend Sparkle. She was the fairy of the Silver Stream that wound its way through the Black Forest. He was on his way to find her, to ask if she knew what had caused all the colours in the sky.

As Michael walked through the forest he realised that he could hear someone crying. He stopped and listened and then, through the trees, he could see a little figure sitting under a tree.

'Poor little fellow,' said Michael to himself as he went to him.

'Hello,' he said softly, 'can I help you?'

Evergreen, because of course the little figure was Evergreen, looked up at him.

'Who are you?' he asked.

'Oh, I am Michael. I live here,' he said. 'I am a leprechaun, you know.' He was very proud of that and liked to tell everyone.

'What is your name?' asked Michael as he sat down beside his new friend.

'Evergreen,' answered the elf.

'Did you see all those colours in the sky?' Michael asked.

Evergreen nodded his head. 'My friend Pinefloat and I put them up there. It was a Rainbow. Well, it would have been if it hadn't been hit by that lightning.'

'It looked very pretty,' remarked Michael.

'Pinefloat was still on it when it fell apart,' Evergreen said.

'Don't worry. He'll be all right, he'll just fly down,' said Michael.

'But we are both elves. We can't fly,' said Evergreen in a forlorn voice.

'I can't either,' said Michael, 'but, Sparkle can,' he added with a smile.

Evergreen looked at Michael. 'Will you help me, Michael? You see, I don't know what to do or where to go.'

'Of course I will help you,' said Michael. 'It's my job. Sparkle and I try to help anyone who is in trouble in our Black Forest. Well, it isn't really our forest, but we like helping others. Our magic would be wasted if we didn't.'

'Do you think that we will find Pinefloat?' Evergreen asked anxiously.

'I hope so,' replied Michael. He thought for a moment and then he said, 'We must see Sparkle. She will know what to do.'

The two little figures set off through the Black Forest towards the Silver Stream.

They hadn't been walking long when Michael began to feel hungry.

'Would you like something to eat?' he asked Evergreen, 'I know where there is a nice strawberry patch, not far from here.'

Evergreen smiled. 'Yes please Michael. I am feeling hungry and I like strawberries very much.'

They soon arrived at the strawberry patch and it wasn't long before they had eaten a lot of strawberries. After a while they stopped eating and turned their meal into a game. They were trying to see which one of them could find the biggest strawberry. The strawberry patch was filled with shouts of 'Look at this one,' and, 'This one's bigger than that one,' and, 'I can hardly lift this one.'

Soon Michael realised that he was doing all the shouting, for Evergreen was standing quite still, staring under a big leaf. Michael walked over to him.

'Is there anything wrong?' he asked.

Evergreen shook his head and lifted the big leaf, 'Look,' he whispered.

'I have never seen a strawberry like that before,' Michael said.

'That's because it's not a strawberry,' said Evergreen.

'Not a strawberry! Not a strawberry! Of course it's a strawberry! This is a strawberry patch, you know,' Michael said excitedly.

'Yes, I know, but that is not a strawberry,' repeated Evergreen.

'If it isn't a strawberry, then what is it?' asked Michael, by now feeling quite puzzled.

'It is red,' answered Evergreen.

'Red!' exclaimed Michael, 'It looks like a strawberry, a bit brighter perhaps.'

'It is a little red gem,' said Evergreen. 'It is one of the colours from the Rainbow.'

He picked up the little red gem very gently. 'All the colours must be like this,' he said.

'Red,' said Michael.

'No, in a gem shape,' said Evergreen. He began to explain. 'All the colours were little gems before they became the Rainbow. When the Rainbow was broken all the colours must have changed back into gems.'

'The rest of them must be nearby,' said Michael eagerly.

'Yes,' answered Evergreen, 'somewhere in the Black Forest.'

'We must tell Sparkle,' said Michael.

Evergreen agreed and so they left the strawberry patch, with Evergreen carefully holding the little red gem, and made their way to the Silver Stream.

The grass on the banks of the Silver Stream was still wet although the storm had passed, and it had stopped raining hours ago.

'Sparkle lives just here,' said Michael, pointing into the water.

'Doesn't she get wet in there?' asked Evergreen.

'Oh, yes,' answered Michael, with a smile.

They made themselves as comfortable as they could on the wet bank of the Silver Stream and waited. They didn't have to wait long. There was a movement in the depths of the Silver Stream, and a moment later, Sparkle flew out of the water. She flew in two big circles to allow the droplets of water to fall from her wings and then landed beside them. Evergreen just looked at her and held the little red gem close to him. He thought he had seen everything, but Sparkle was something he had not seen before.

Her name was Sparkle because her eyes sparkled as brightly as the ripples on the Silver Stream. She had very large transparent wings and long golden hair. She wore a long blue flowing gown with a white ribbon about her waist. Her magical powers were exceptional, as was her power to fly.

As Evergreen just gazed at her, Michael told her how the Rainbow had been broken and of their adventures in the strawberry patch. Evergreen was suddenly aware of Sparkle's hand touching his.

'We will find Pinefloat and all the other colours too. Don't worry,' she said softly.

Chapter Three -The Pot of Gold

Though everything had happened very quickly, it seemed a very long time since Pinefloat had fallen from the Rainbow. All the colours had gone and the sky was grey again. If he had thought a little bit quicker he could have used his magic to save himself from the fall, but Pinefloat didn't want to lose his pot of gold. He had let it go when the lightning hit the Rainbow and now he was trying to see where it had landed. It was very difficult as he was still falling out of the sky. He hoped that he would land some where soft.

Pinefloat was getting closer and closer to the ground and he could see that he was going to land just inside the Black Forest, in the garden of a little cottage by the side of the Silver Stream. His pot of gold was going to land on the other side of the Silver Stream but Pinefloat couldn't see exactly where.

Then it happened. BUMP! He landed right on top of a big dandelion. The petals were very soft and the flower's pollen went up his nose.

'I am down,' he exclaimed, and then he sneezed.

'Bless you,' said a voice from under the flower. Pinefloat sneezed again and this time he blew himself right out of the dandelion and landed flat on his back on the grass.

'Bless you,' said the voice again.

Pinefloat looked up to see a little elf smiling at him. He wore a suit of light blue with a silver belt and red boots. On his head was a red hat.

'My name is Tassel,' said the elf as he helped Pinefloat to his feet.

'Thank you,' said Pinefloat. 'My name is...is...' His name was lost in another sneeze and Pinefloat found himself flat on his back on the grass again.'...Pinefloat!' he shouted.

'I am very pleased to meet you,' said Tassel as he helped Pinefloat to his feet again. 'Can you stand on your feet now?' he asked.

'Oh yes, thank you,' answered Pinefloat. 'Did you see a pot of gold fall out of the sky?' he asked anxiously, 'It is the only one I have.'

'I did see something come down. It landed on a ledge on the other side of the Silver Stream,' answered Tassel. He paused and then said, 'How did it come to be in the sky?'

'Oh, it's a long story,' said Pinefloat, 'I was sliding down a Rainbow with a pot of gold.'

'A Rainbow?' interrupted Tassel.

'Yes, a Rainbow. My friend Evergreen and I put seven colours into the sky to cheer everyone up after the storm, and it was hit by lightning before I had a chance to put the pot of gold at the end of it.'

'Oh,' said Tassel, for he had never seen a Rainbow.

'Most of the colours landed before I did,' Pinefloat went on. 'They looked as if they fell into the Black Forest.'

'The Black Forest?' repeated Tassel.

'Yes,' said Pinefloat.

Tassel had listened intently to Pinefloat's story and couldn't wait to help.

'How do you feel after your fall?' inquired Tassel.

'I am all right, thank you. The dandelion saved me,' answered Pinefloat. 'I have stopped sneezing now too,' he added.

'I think I know where your pot of gold is,' said Tassel, 'I have a boat, it is tied to some reeds just over there,' Tassel was pointing at the Silver Stream.

27

'If you wait for me there, I will get some ropes from the cottage and we will get the pot of gold back.'

Tassel went into the cottage, and Pinefloat walked through the garden to the Silver Stream. It wasn't long before Tassel joined him and they were soon crossing the Silver Stream in the little brown boat. As they approached the other side, Pinefloat could see the ledge that Tassel had told him about.

'It's very high,' remarked Pinefloat.

Tassel expertly brought the boat to a stop just under the ledge. He tied it to an overhanging branch and when it was secure, he sat down.

'It is going to be difficult,' said Tassel. 'As you can see, the bank is so steep just here that we can't step out of the boat onto it.'

'How will we get up to the ledge?' asked Pinefloat.

'We use the ropes,' said Tassel.

'I could wish myself up there,' said Pinefloat.

'You know that you must only grant wishes to others,' Tassel reminded him.

No more was said on the subject and it wasn't long before the two elves were climbing the steep bank to the ledge. It took a lot of strength to climb all that way, but soon they were standing on the ledge, the little brown boat bobbing about on the Silver Stream below them.

They looked around and at first they couldn't see anything, and then, half buried in the ground, Pinefloat found the pot of gold.

'Here it is!' he called excitedly.

Tassel ran over to look. Yes, sure enough it was the pot of gold, a little bit dented but all there. They dug it out of the ground and walked back to the ledge. Tassel tied the rope to the pot of gold and lowered it down into his boat. Then the two elves climbed down the steep bank and seated them selves in the boat. Tassel untied the boat from the overhanging branch and they sailed back across the

Silver Stream.

When they reached the other side, Tassel made the boat secure and he and Pinefloat climbed out and walked through the garden to the little cottage. It was beginning to get dark and so they decided that Pinefloat would stay in the cottage with Tassel for the night.

Once inside the cottage, the two elves made their way to the attic. This was where Tassel slept. From the window they could see the garden and the Silver Stream.

'This is a very nice place,' said Pinefloat.

'Yes it is,' agreed Tassel.

'I must try to find my friend Evergreen tomorrow.'

'I will take you in my boat,' said Tassel.

'Oh, thank you!' said Pinefloat. He paused and then asked, 'Do you know the way?'

'Of course, we will take my boat and sail upstream, and we will soon find your friend,' said Tassel.

Soon it was very dark and the two new friends slept soundly. The night passed quickly and the two elves were awake very early the next morning. After breakfast Pinefloat and Tassel made their way through the cottage and into the garden. It was cold. There was dew all over the grass and a thick mist covered the Silver Stream.

When the two elves had boarded the boat, Tassel hoisted the white sail and began to steer it upstream, moving slowly through the mist. Pinefloat spent most of the journey polishing the pot of gold, while Tassel did his best to see through the mist which was still quite thick.

They travelled on and on and just as the sun was beginning to shine through the clouds, the mist began to lift.

'We must be close to finding Evergreen,' said Pinefloat.

'I think we have quite a way to go,' answered Tassel.

Pinefloat put down the pot of gold and waited patiently as the boat sailed on upstream.

'This must be a magical place,' said Pinefloat.

'Yes it is.' answered Tassel.

Chapter Four - Blue

Sparkle was the most beautiful fairy that Evergreen had ever seen, and he had seen many. She was dressed in a blue flowing gown with a white ribbon about her waist and she was talking to Michael.

'It must be one of the colours,' she was saying, 'it's at the bottom of the stream, tangled up in all the weeds.'

'Shall we swim down and get it?' asked Michael.

'Can you swim?' Sparkle asked Evergreen.

'Oh, yes,' he answered. 'Is it very deep?' he asked.

'Not too deep,' said Sparkle reassuringly. She flew into the air and dived into the water.

'Sometimes I think I would like to be able to fly,' said Michael.

Evergreen agreed with him and the leprechaun and the elf dived into the water after Sparkle.

It was cold in the water and it grew colder as they dived deeper. When they reached the bottom, Sparkle was already untangling the weeds around a glittering object. Michael and Evergreen swam over to help her. The object was almost free when Michael signalled that he was going back up. Evergreen did the same and they left Sparkle to pull away the last of the weeds.

When Michael and Evergreen reached the surface of the Silver Stream they swam to the edge and climbed out. Side by side, they sat on the bank and watched the water.

'Sparkle has been down there a long time,' said Evergreen, 'do you think she is all right?'

'She lives in the stream,' answered Michael, 'I don't know how she breathes down there. I have to come up for air.'

30

'So do I,' said Evergreen.

Just as he said this, Sparkle appeared. 'I have taken it to my Magical Cave,' she said. 'Will you both come down and look at it?'

Michael and Evergreen dived into the water and followed Sparkle down to her Magical Cave. Although Michael had known Sparkle for a very long time, he had never been to her underwater Magical Cave before. It was a place of enchantment, even for a leprechaun and an elf.

All though Evergreen had been everywhere and seen everything, he had never seen a place like this.

'Do you like it?' asked Sparkle.

'Yes, very much,' said Michael.

'Oh yes, it's...it's lovely,' added Evergreen.

He was having difficulty finding words for this magical place. The Magical Cave was filled with air and was really quite big. There was a small hole in the top that let light in, but was well hidden in the roots of a big willow tree. One side of the Magical Cave faced the Silver Stream, this also let in light. This was how Sparkle entered and left her Magical Cave. The Magical Cave was a very magical place and this is why the Silver Stream never flooded in to it. The Magical Cave was sphere-shaped and the walls were sprinkled with sparkling pieces of gold and silver. There was a small table with two chairs and a large mirror.

'Here it is,' said Sparkle, holding up the object that she had taken from the bed of the Silver Stream.

'It's blue!' exclaimed Evergreen.

'Is it one of your colours?' asked Sparkle.

'Yes, it is, it looks like a little blue gem, just like the little red one that I left on the bank,' said Evergreen.

'Would you like to leave your colours here until you have found them all?' asked Sparkle.

'Yes please,' Evergreen answered.

'I will fetch the red colour,' said Sparkle. 'You look around the Magical Cave if you want to.'

'Thank you,' said Michael and Evergreen together. A moment later Sparkle was gone.

Michael and Evergreen started to look around the Magical Cave. It was a very lovely place indeed. In one part of the Magical Cave there were stone things that looked like icicles hanging from the ceiling and some growing up from the floor. There was a pool of crystal clear water and a tiny beam of sunlight that shone from the small hole in the roof.

'She spends a lot of time down here,' said Michael.

Just then, Sparkle arrived with the little red gem. She moved closer to the leprechaun and the elf and picked up the blue gem.

'Two,' she said, holding up the red gem and the blue gem side by side. 'How many are there?' she asked.

'Seven,' answered Evergreen.

Sparkle put the two colours down on the flat circular stone that she used as a table. 'Shall we see if we can find any more colours?' she asked.

Michael and Evergreen nodded their heads in agreement, and so they left the Magical Cave.

When Michael and Evergreen reached the surface of the Silver Stream, Sparkle was flying in little circles above them. Michael reached the bank and climbed out of the water. He looked around for Evergreen but he wasn't there. Then Michael heard Sparkle calling to him, 'Evergreen has been caught in the current and is being taken downstream!'

Michael ran along the bank of the Silver Stream, but Evergreen was moving too fast. Sparkle flew just above Evergreen but she wasn't strong enough to pull him out of the water. In less than a moment, Evergreen was out of sight, and Sparkle was back on the bank with Michael.

'We have lost him,' she said.

'What can we do?' asked Michael.

'I don't know,' answered Sparkle.

The two little people tried to comfort each other as they gazed at the water that had carried their friend away.

Chapter Five - Green

Evergreen struggled for a long time in the water to reach the bank of the Silver Stream, but the current was too strong for him. He grabbed a piece of wood that was caught in the current with him to help him stay afloat, but he was carried on downstream.

It was now evening and slowly getting dark. Soon night would come. Evergreen knew that he had to get out of the water. He was just thinking of using some magic to do it when, without warning, the Silver Stream rushed around a bend and pushed him and his piece of wood into the reeds that grew on the bank.

As Evergreen climbed thankfully out of the water, he saw something shining in the grass just above him. He reached out and picked it up.

'Green,' he said.

He looked at the little green gem for a while, and then realised that it was getting very dark all around him. So he climbed into the branches of a tree and was soon asleep. The little elf slept so well that it was mid-morning when he awoke. There had been a mist over the stream but now it was completely gone.

Evergreen reached into his pocket and took out the little green gem. He looked at it and smiled. Then something else caught his eye. It was a little brown boat with a white sail. It was pushing its way upstream. Evergreen put the gem back into his pocket and watched as the boat came closer. As it did, he couldn't believe his eyes, for in the boat with another little elf was his friend, Pinefloat. He quickly climbed out of the tree and as the boat came closer he shouted, 'Pinefloat! Pinefloat! Over here! It's me! Evergreen!'

Pinefloat could see Evergreen standing on the bank and said excitedly to Tassel, 'That's my friend Evergreen! Will you stop the boat so that he can come aboard?'

Tassel sailed the boat to the bank and Evergreen climbed in.

'Evergreen, this is Tassel. He helped me to find the pot of gold, after I had lost it, when I fell off the Rainbow.'

Evergreen said, 'Thank you Tassel, for bringing my friend back to me.'

Then he put his hand in his pocket and brought out the little green gem.

'Green!' exclaimed Pinefloat.

'Yes,' said Evergreen, 'and I have found two new friends, Michael and Sparkle, they helped me to find red and blue.'

'Where are Michael and Sparkle?' asked Tassel.

'Oh, they are further upstream,' answered Evergreen. 'You see, I was caught in the fast moving current of the stream yesterday afternoon and...'

'I am sorry to interrupt,' said Tassel. 'Shall I sail on?' he asked.

'Yes please,' answered Pinefloat.

Tassel manoeuvred the little brown boat away from the bank and they continued on there way. Evergreen told Pinefloat all about his adventures while Tassel sailed the boat, and then Pinefloat told Evergreen all about his adventures. Tassel just sailed the boat, and listened to both of them.

It was approaching midday, and Evergreen and Pinefloat had long since stopped talking. The voyage had been very peaceful until Evergreen said, 'A Rainbow is not a good idea!'

'Of course it is!' said Pinefloat.

Before Tassel knew what was happening, they were arguing again.

'It is!' argued Pinefloat.

'It isn't!' replied Evergreen.

So it went on, until Tassel brought the boat to a stop close to the grassy bank.

'We have arrived,' he said, 'Sparkle lives here.'

Tassel was pointing at the water. He manoeuvred the boat a little closer to the bank and tied it to some reeds.

'Where are they?' asked Pinefloat.

'Looking for me, I suspect,' answered Evergreen.

'When they realise that they will not find me, they will come back here.'

'We'll wait for them,' said Tassel.

They didn't have long to wait before the leprechaun and the fairy of the Silver Stream returned and, once they had all been introduced, Sparkle suggested that they should take the little green gem, and the pot of gold, to her underwater Magical Cave. So it was agreed and soon they all stood in the Magical Cave admiring the red, blue, and green gems, which lay next to the pot of gold on Sparkle's round stone table.

Chapter Six - Orange

Sparkle, Michael, Tassel, Evergreen and Pinefloat had all spent a peaceful night in Sparkle's Magical Cave. It was now early morning and the mist had lifted from the Silver Stream. It wasn't long before the little people had left the Magical Cave and were standing on the bank of the Silver Stream. They had decided to look for the other colours.

'It might be best if we split up to look for the colours, we can meet back here this evening,' said Michael.

So after everyone had said goodbye, they all set off in different directions. Sparkle flew into the air and would look for the colours from above. Evergreen would go up stream and Pinefloat would go down. Tassel would look in the forest on one side of the Silver Stream and Michael would look in the forest on the other.

It was on the other side of the Silver Stream that the Black Castle stood, and in it lived the Black Witch. Michael tried never to go near the Black Castle, but he said he would search for the colours on this side of the forest, and that was what he intended to do.

He looked under mushrooms and through all the long grass, he looked in rabbit holes and under the trees. As midday approached, he found himself outside the walls of the Black Castle. He crept quietly past the Black Castle as he didn't want to attract the attention of the Black Witch. He was soon on the other side of the Black Castle, and just about to continue his search when he heard a noise. It was the sound of a bird, and it sounded as if it needed help.

'Where are you?' Michael asked.

He heard the bird again, and so he walked in the direction of the sound. As he pushed some of the undergrowth out of the way, a bird with black and white feathers came into view.

'Can I help?' asked Michael.

The bird just looked at him.

'Excuse me, one moment,' said Michael as he waved is hand in the air, using only a fragment of the magic power he possessed.

'Try to speak now,' he said to the bird.

'Thank you,' said the bird.

'Are you hurt?' enquired Michael.

'Yes,' said the bird, 'I was flying to my nest and a very strong gust of wind blew me into a tree. I think my wing is broken.'

'Do you mind if I have a look at it?' asked Michael.

'Please do,' replied the bird.

Michael very carefully opened the wing of the black and white bird.

'You're a magpie, aren't you?' he enquired.

'Yes, that's right,' came the reply. 'Is it broken?'

Michael looked very thoughtful and then replied.

'Yes. Yes it is.'

The magpie knew that he would never be able to fly again, and he was very sad.

'I think I can help you,' said Michael cheerfully.

He took hold of the magpie's wing and closed his eyes. The magpie felt his wing tingling, and a moment later Michael opened his eyes and let go of the bird's wing.

'Try that,' he said.

The bird opened his wings and then closed them again.

'It's mended!' the magpie said with delight.

'Oh, good. It worked!' exclaimed Michael.

'But how did you...?' Michael interrupted him, 'I am a leprechaun,' he said with a smile.

'Is there anything I can do for you?' asked the magpie.

'I don't think so, thank you,' said Michael. 'That is unless you have seen any little coloured gems?'

'I found something that looked like a gem this morning,' said the magpie. 'It's in my nest. Would you like to see it?'

'Yes please,' answered Michael.

No sooner had he spoken than the bird had flown high into a nearby tree. A moment or two passed and the magpie returned with something shining in its beak. He dropped it on the soft green grass.

'Is that it?' asked the bird.

Michael didn't know what colour it was, but it shone just like the other colours he had seen. 'Yes, I think so,' he replied.

'Then it's yours,' said the magpie.

Michael picked it up and put it into his pocket, 'Thank you very much,' he said.

'Is there anything else that I can do?' asked the magpie.

Michael paused and then said, 'If it's not too much trouble, would you fly me back to the Silver Stream? I wouldn't like to walk past the Black Castle again.'

'Of course I will,' answered the bird. 'Climb aboard.'

No sooner was Michael seated between the bird's wings than he was in the air looking down on the Black Castle. He noticed something on one of the towers that looked like another colour, but he said nothing, and soon the magpie landed by the Silver Stream. Michael climbed down to the ground and thanked the bird. He watched as the magpie took to the air again and soon it was lost from his sight.

The afternoon passed quickly and when Michael reached Sparkle's Magical Cave the others were waiting for him, that is, all except Evergreen. As he approached them he took the little gem from his pocket.

'Orange!' exclaimed Pinefloat.

Michael gave the little gem to Sparkle. She flew into the air holding the orange light so that they could all see it, then she dived into the Silver Stream.

Sparkle was in the underwater Magical Cave for some time and when she returned to the others, there was still no sign of Evergreen.

'Perhaps we should take the boat and look for him,' said Tassel.

'He was all right when I saw him this afternoon,' said Sparkle, 'he was just about to collect one of the little gems from a water lily.'

Chapter Seven - Pink

Evergreen had followed the Silver Stream until he came upon a large log lying across the water that had made it become almost still, and the Silver Stream had widened until it looked like a small pond. In the middle of this pond was a cluster of water lilies. Evergreen sat down on the bank and gazed at them. Then something caught his eye. Nestling on one of the flowers, something was shining.

'Pink!' exclaimed Evergreen with a smile.

Sure enough, the little pink gem was lodged on one of the lilies. Evergreen dived into the Silver Stream and swam to the water lilies. He looked inside each one until he found the one with the shining gem in it. He couldn't quite reach the little gem from the water, so he tried to climb onto the leaves that were floating around the lilies.

Somehow, he lost his grip on the flower petals and fell back into the water. He went right under and then bobbed up again, just like a little cork. But when he came up, the sky was gone. He found himself in a very small space under one of the big leaves.

At first he was very frightened, but then he decided that he would just make a hole in the leaf. He tried hitting the leaf with his hand, but it was too thick. He was still trapped, and so he began to feel afraid again.

Just then, a newt came swimming by, and popped up into the little air pocket in which Evergreen was trapped.

'Hello,' said Evergreen, trying not to sound frightened.

The newt said nothing, so Evergreen used a little bit of magic.

'Hello,' he said again.

'Hello,' answered the newt. 'What are you doing here?'

'I'm trying to get to the other side of the leaf,' answered Evergreen.

'Why don't you use some magic?' asked the newt.

'I am not supposed to use my magic to help myself,' said Evergreen. 'But if I don't get out of here soon, I will.'

'Why don't you swim out?' asked the newt.

'I don't know which way to swim, and I don't know if I can hold my breath long enough,' answered Evergreen.

'I will help you,' said the newt.

Before Evergreen had time to say anything, the newt was gone. He soon returned and with him he brought two small sharp stones from the bottom of the Silver Stream. He gave them to Evergreen. Evergreen took them and soon cut a hole in the leaf big enough to climb through.

He thanked the newt and climbed through the hole and out of the water. He was now right next to the flower with the little pink gem lodged in it. He reached out and pulled it from the flower. As soon as it was safely in his pocket, Evergreen dived back into the water and swam back to the bank.

When, at last, he was standing on the bank, he took the pink gem from his pocket and looked at it. The little elf smiled, for although he had been very frightened, he was now extremely happy as he walked beside the Silver Stream back to Sparkle's Magical Cave.

When he arrived he found Michael, Sparkle, Pinefloat and Tassel waiting for him on the bank of the Silver Stream.

'I have found one,' said Evergreen triumphantly holding the little pink gem in the air.

'I have found one too,' said Michael.

'It was Orange,' added Pinefloat.

Evergreen gave the little gem to Sparkle who promptly dived into the Silver Stream with it.

'That makes five we have found,' said Evergreen.

'There must be two more somewhere,' remarked Pinefloat.

'Yes,' agreed Evergreen, it was the first time in a long time that the two little elves had agreed on anything. Evergreen was thinking about his adventure under the lily's leaves, and wondering if he would have helped himself with magic, if he had been unable to escape.

Evening was throwing a dark cloak over the forest, and so the little people dived into the Silver Stream and swam down to Sparkle's Magical Cave for the night.

Tomorrow they would go in search of the last two missing colours.

Chapter Eight - Yellow

Michael was first to awaken. It was very early and he had remembered something. He sat quite still and waited for the others to wake up. He didn't have to wait long and once his companions were all awake, he said, 'I know where there is another colour. I saw it yesterday.'

They all looked at him. 'Where did you see it?' asked Sparkle.

Michael paused and then he said, 'On top of one of the towers of the Black Castle, I think the Black Witch is using it as a light.'

'We'll just have to ask her to give it back to us,' said Evergreen. 'Won't we?' He gave Pinefloat a nudge.

'Yes,' said Pinefloat.

'If the Black Witch has one of your colours, it won't be that easy to get it back,' Sparkle told them.

'I think we ought to try,' said Evergreen.

So they agreed and the little people left Sparkle's Magical Cave to make their way to the Black Castle. It was mid morning when they arrived and, sure enough, one of the little gems was on top of one of the towers.

'Yellow!' exclaimed Pinefloat.

Evergreen and Pinefloat walked boldly up to the big door of the Black Castle and knocked upon it. Sparkle and Tassel stayed out of sight in the shadows of the trees. Michael said, 'I am just going to see a friend. I won't be long,' and he walked off into the Black Forest.

The big wooden door opened and there stood the Black Witch.

Even now, at midday, she looked as black as night. Evergreen spoke. Pinefloat stood behind him.

'I am very sorry to bother you, but...'

'Go on. Ask her,' urged Pinefloat.

'Ask me? Ask me what?' said the Black Witch as she stepped into the sunlight.

'The little gem on your tower is ours, and we wondered if you would give it back to us,' said Evergreen with uncertainty.

'Give it back? Give it back? Be off with you or I will lock you both up in my dungeons!' shouted the Black Witch, her voice echoing through the Black Castle. Evergreen and Pinefloat ran from the door as she slammed it shut. They soon reached the shelter of the trees where Sparkle and Tassel were waiting for them.

'She said no,' said Evergreen.

'She said that she was going to lock us up,' added Pinefloat. Then they realised that Michael wasn't there and both together they asked, 'Where is Michael?'

'He said he was going to see a friend,' answered Sparkle.

The four little people sat on the grass beneath a tree and looked up at the tower with the little yellow gem on it.

'You could fly up there and get it,' Pinefloat said to Sparkle.

'I would if I could,' the fairy answered, 'but only the Black Witch's magic works inside the Black Castle. As soon as I fly over the castle walls my magic would be gone and I would fall, like an acorn from an oak tree, to the ground.'

Then a black and white bird flew into view. It flew to the Black Castles tower and landed. It waited a moment and then flew into the air again. The little yellow gem was gone from the tower and the bird flew down to the ground. Michael jumped down from the bird's back and it flew up into the sky and away. Michael walked over to his friends, in his hand he held the little yellow gem.

'She wouldn't give it to you, would she?' he said.

'No,' said Pinefloat.

Michael gave him the yellow gem, 'One more to find,' he said.

'Oh, we know where it is,' said Evergreen.

'Well, let's get it,' said Michael impatiently.

'It's around the Black Witch's neck,' said Evergreen grimly.

'She won't give you that one back either,' said Michael.

'She might take it off at night,' suggested Tassel.

'Our magic powers won't work inside the Black Castle,' Michael pointed out. 'We will have to be very careful and make sure we are not caught.'

So they made their plan, they would wait until nightfall and then creep into the Black Castle to try to recover the last colour, purple.

Chapter Nine - Purple

As evening came, darkness swiftly covered the Black Forest. The Black Castle looked even more frightening in its darkened shroud, and the little people were reluctant to enter it. But, they knew that if they wanted the last colour back, then they must go in. It would be a very dangerous night for all of them, as they would have no magical powers to help them.

They left the shelter of the trees and walked to the big wooden door. They tried to open it, but it was locked.

'This will be the last magic we can use until we are back outside again,' Sparkle said, as she waved her hand in the air. They heard the locks on the door rumbling and then the door opened just a little. They looked at one another and then pushed the door just a little more, and crept inside the Black Castle.

Michael led the way. He took them across the courtyard and through a door at the other side. Tassel, Sparkle, Evergreen and Pinefloat followed him along dark passageways, and down stone steps, until at last, in a dimly lit room that could have been a dungeon in the heart of the Black Castle they found the Black Witch. She was sitting in a big black chair, the little purple gem still around her neck.

It had taken quite a long time to find the Black Witch and it was now almost midnight. The Black Witch sensed that she was not alone and looked up to see the five little people looking at her. She rose to her feet.

'What are you doing in my castle?' she asked in a loud voice.

Evergreen tried to tell her, but he was so frightened that the words wouldn't come out of his mouth.

'What do you want?' she said in an even louder voice.

Pinefloat tried to answer her. 'We came to ask...'

The Black Witch didn't let him finish. 'I told you. NO!' Her voice echoed around the room and along the stone passageways. 'I also told you that I would lock you up.' Her voice was a little softer, but her words were followed by a loud burst of thunder.

Evergreen and Pinefloat held on to each other and waited for something to happen. They both wished that the Black Witch would disappear, but she didn't. Instead she began to walk towards them.

'You have our colour around your neck...' Pinefloat's voice was drowned out by another roar of thunder, followed by the Black Witch.

'Your colour? Your colour?' Her voice was getting louder every time she said something. 'You mean MY colour!' she shouted.

Evergreen and Pinefloat backed away from her but she came after them. To make things difficult for her, they split up. Evergreen went to one side of the dungeon and Pinefloat went to the other.

'It's not your colour,' Sparkle said softly.

The Black Witch looked at the little fairy. 'It's not yours either!' she shouted. The Black Witch took the purple gem in her hand and pulled it from her neck. 'I can destroy you with it,' she screamed. 'You are no stronger than butterflies in my castle!' She laughed an uncontrollable wicked laugh as a deafening peal of thunder echoed around the Black Castle. She looked at the little purple gem and then hurled it at Sparkle with all her might. 'TAKE IT!' screamed the Black Witch.

Sparkle was so frightened that she couldn't move. She covered her face with her hands and watched through her fingers as the ball of light raced towards her. Then she saw Tassel step in front of her. His voice seemed loud in the room. 'No! I command that you find another path!' He pointed at the flying gem that was hurtling through the air towards him. He summoned up all his strength, and in doing so, used some magic from somewhere. He knew it wasn't his, yet it was helping him. As the tiny light was almost upon him, it obeyed his command. It was so close to him that it couldn't find another path, so instead, it broke into two. In doing so, its colour changed very slightly. There were now two little gems, both the same colour but one a little brighter than the other. They passed, one either side of Tassel and Sparkle. As they did, suddenly there were two other figures with them in the dungeon.

Tassel's shadow jumped from the wall and his reflection rose from the wet floor. The shadow caught one of the small gems and his reflection caught the other. The two phantoms gave the coloured gems to Tassel, their eyes flashed with gold and then they vanished from sight. The Black Witch couldn't believe what she had seen.

'Run!' shouted Michael.

The five little people turned and ran from the dungeon. They ran back the way they had come, up stone steps, along dark passages, across the courtyard and through the big wooden door. At last they were safe outside. It was raining and flashes of lightning filled the sky.

'What happened back there in the Black Castle?' asked Michael.

'I really don't know,' answered Tassel, 'I gave the command and something else answered me. It wasn't my magic.'

'Who were the other two figures?' asked Michael.

'They were my shadow and my reflection,' answered Tassel. 'Did you notice that they both had gold-coloured eyes,' he said. As yet the little people could not know of the existence of the Ice Crystal.

It was too dangerous to stay near the Black Castle, so the five little people walked through the Black Forest in the rain. Soon they would be back at Sparkle's Magical Cave and they would be glad to be there.

Chapter Ten - The Rainbow

The storm had raged all night, the lightning lit up the sky and the thunder rumbled around in the clouds, echoing through the Black Forest. The sun was just rising and trying to look through the grey clouds when Michael, Sparkle, Evergreen, Pinefloat and Tassel arrived back at Sparkle's Magical Cave. It had been a long walk through the Black Forest in the rain, and the five little people were very glad to be back.

At last all the little gems were on Sparkle's round stone table, and the Magical Cave was filled with colours reflected from them.

'When the storm is over we can make another Rainbow,' said Evergreen.

'Oh no!' said Pinefloat. 'We have tried once and almost lost all our colours, and our pot of gold.'

'But we must! The Rainbow was going to cheer everyone up after the storm,' said Evergreen.

'It didn't work last time!' replied Pinefloat.

'It will this time,' said a soft voice. It was Sparkle. 'If you would like to make another Rainbow, I think I can help.'

'We used magic bubbles last time,' said Evergreen enthusiastically.

'If I think of a way to put the colours into the sky, will you both agree?' asked Sparkle.

They both said 'Yes,' together.

The little people were very tired after their very busy night. Sparkle suggested that they all tried to sleep until the storm was over. So they all settled down to sleep, all except Sparkle. She wandered around her Magical Cave, first looking at the entrance, which was always under water, then at the mirror, then at the clear crystal pool. The sunbeam wasn't shining into it this morning, but that was because the sky was still very grey and cloudy.

Sparkle had an idea. She knew how to put the colours into the sky. She also knew that when the sunbeam shone into the clear crystal pool, it would be time to make the Rainbow.

As mid-morning approached the storm began to ease. The thunder and lightning stopped, but it continued to rain. The sun at last began to peep through the grey clouds, and in Sparkle's Magical Cave the sunbeam once more shone on to the clear crystal pool. The time had come.

Very quietly she went to each of her friends and woke them up. 'It is time,' she said.

'Have you thought of a way to put the colours into the sky?' asked Evergreen.

'Yes, I have,' answered Sparkle.

'But first we need a Crystal Prism, with lots of shining surfaces.'

'I'll make one,' volunteered Evergreen. No sooner had he said it, than he had made it. 'Is this all right? he asked.

The crystal was sphere-shaped with lots of shining flat surfaces. Sparkle smiled. 'It is just right,' she said. 'Now place it at the Magical Cave's entrance, so that it will shine into the Silver Stream.'

Evergreen placed it very carefully next to the watery entrance. Michael, Tassel and Pinefloat, watched intently. Sparkle continued with her instructions.

'Now take one colour at a time and push it gently into the Crystal Prism.'

Evergreen carefully picked up the little red gem and moved across the Magical Cave. He pushed it gently into the Crystal Prism without damaging it, then went back to the round table to collect another colour. He was about to pick one up when Pinefloat arrived beside him.

'I will help you to put them into the Crystal Prism,' he said. Pinefloat picked up the green gem and Evergreen picked up the blue one, and together they crossed the Magical Cave and pushed the two colours into the Crystal Prism. As they turned to walk back to the table, they were met by Michael and Tassel who were each holding a colour. Michael handed the orange gem to Evergreen and Tassel handed the pink gem to Pinefloat. The two elves pushed the colours into the Crystal Prism. Evergreen, Pinefloat and Michael were joined by Sparkle who was holding the yellow gem, she pushed it into the Crystal Prism. Evergreen and Pinefloat went back to the table to collect the two remaining colours. When they returned they had started arguing again.

'It was purple!' stated Evergreen.

'Well it isn't now!' said Pinefloat.

'They look lighter than purple,' said Evergreen calmly, 'but not as light as blue,'

'We can't call them blue,' said Pinefloat.

'We can't call them purple either!' added Evergreen.

'No, we can't,' agreed Pinefloat, 'because they aren't, any more!'

'We have to call them something,' said Evergreen.

Tassel interrupted them. 'May I give them a name?' he asked.

Evergreen and Pinefloat looked at each other.

'Tassel did cause purple to change into whatever they are now,' Michael reminded them.

Tassel took the little gem from Evergreen and said, 'This one is indigo.' He pushed it into the Crystal Prism. Then he took the other gem from Pinefloat. He looked at it for a moment, 'This one is violet,' he said. Then he pushed the last colour into the Crystal Prism.

'Now they are ready to go into the sky,' said Sparkle, as she moved to the clear crystal pool. 'Will you all stand back, please,' she said.

The three elves and the leprechaun moved away from the colour-filled Crystal Prism and watched Sparkle.

'Tassel will you help me to move the mirror?' she asked.

Tassel and Sparkle took the mirror that was next to her table, from the wall of the Magical Cave. They gently pushed it into the sunbeam, stopping it vanishing into the crystal clear pool of water. Instead it was now reflected into the Crystal Prism. As soon as the sunlight hit the Crystal Prism, it reflected the colours out of the Magical Cave and into the Silver Stream.

'The colours are leaving,' said Evergreen.

'Yes,' said Sparkle with smile.

For once the five little people used their magic to help

themselves. They vanished from the Magical Cave and reappeared on the bank of the Silver Stream. They had never seen a Rainbow, and so they watched as the colours rose from the Silver Stream.

Up, up, up they went, right up into the sky, and then they bowed and started to fall, leaving a trail of colours behind them.

'Where do we bury the pot of gold?' asked Pinefloat.

'We'll leave it in the Magical Cave,' answered Sparkle. 'A Rainbow has two ends,' she added with a smile.

So, one of the loveliest and most wonderful things in the world hung in the sky, watched by the little people who had put it there: The Rainbow Makers.

4. The Moon Fairy

Chapter One

Far away, just at a place where the land meets the sea, there is a little cottage with a big garden. This was no ordinary cottage, for in it lived an elf, his name was Tassel. He shared the cottage with a man, a woman, and their two children.

Tassel had lived in the cottage for many years. He had many adventures, and had watched the two babies grow into children. He enjoyed their games and often listened to the bedtime stories their mother told them.

It was a bedtime story night the first time Tassel introduced himself to the children's mother. He was in such terrible trouble and he asked the lady if she could help him. She knew about fairies, elves and magic things, and she did help him. Tassel had promised to grant the lady three wishes.

Tassel had made his way to the children's bedroom. Tonight when the children were asleep, he was going to keep his promise. He listened to the bedtime story and the little song the children sang, but it wasn't long before silence fell over the bedroom. It was time, so Tassel spoke, 'Excuse me, over here.'

The lady looked around the bedroom and then she saw the tiny figure standing on the bedside table. He was dressed in blue with a red hat and red boots. Around his waist was a silver belt.

'I have returned to keep my promise, I will grant you three wishes.'

The lady smiled at him. 'Thank you, but I'm not in need of any wishes.'

'If not for you, is there anything I can do for the children?' asked Tassel.

She thought for a moment and then she smiled. 'Yes, yes there is.'

'Make your wishes,' Tassel whispered.

'I would like to wish for three things for both children, is that all right?' she asked.

'It is, make your wishes,' Tassel said again.

The lady closed her eyes and clasped her hands together. 'I wish for health, hope, and happiness, for both children to last all their lives.' The lady opened her eyes and looked anxiously at the little elf.

'Your wishes have been granted,' he said softly, then he vanished, leaving no trace that he had ever been with her at all.

Many years passed and Tassel had many adventures and made new friends. Two little people became very good friends, they were Michael and Sparkle.

Michael was a leprechaun and he lived in the Black Forest. He was just a bit bigger than most fairy folk. He had a beaming face and always wore a smile, well almost always. He was dressed in emerald green with brown boots and a brown belt with a gold buckle. He was a happy fellow but never as happy as when he was with Sparkle, the fairy of the Silver Stream.

Sparkle lived in an underwater Magical Cave in the Silver Stream that wound its way through the Black Forest. She was named Sparkle because her eyes sparkled as brightly as the ripples on the Silver Stream when the sun shone upon them.

She had very large transparent wings and long golden hair. She usually wore a long blue flowing gown, but sometimes this was changed for a white one. Her magical powers were exceptional as was her power to fly. She spent most of her time with Michael, and together they looked after the Black Forest, and all the creatures who lived in it.

Sometimes Tassel would come to stay with Michael and Sparkle. He would sail his little brown boat upstream into the Black Forest, and help them with the things that had to be done to make the Black Forest a good place to be.

Tassel had many adventures with Michael and Sparkle, but he didn't know that one day his very existence would depend on his friends.

Although many years had passed, Tassel, as with all fairy folk, did not change in appearance. But, the children had grown older and the older they grew the more grown up they became. Slowly, unknown to Tassel, they stopped believing in fairies. This was going to bring more trouble to Tassel than anyone could imagine.

Chapter Two

It was a hot summer day, Tassel had sailed his little brown boat with its white sail upstream into the Black Forest. Today he wore a suit of light blue with a silver belt and red boots. On his head he wore a red hat. He was on his way to visit Michael and Sparkle, he hoped to take them on a picnic.

Before he was able to find them, he began to feel very dizzy. Losing his balance, he fell off his seat and lay in the bottom of his boat. Tassel looked up at the sky, through the trees. In his head he could hear a voice.

'I summon you to come to me. NOW!'

'Who are you?' Tassel asked aloud.

'I am the Goblin King. Come to me now. I command it.'

Tassel's head began to clear and when he could sit up he realised his boat was stuck on the bank of the Silver Stream. In the distance he could hear voices. He secured his boat and walked through the Black Forest in the direction of the voices. Soon he arrived at a clearing. In the centre surrounded by goblins was the Goblin King. When Tassel entered the clearing a quiet stillness fell over the Black Forest. The goblins turned to face him, and the Goblin King spoke.

'You have come. Good! Come closer to me, Tassel.'

Tassel walked slowly towards the Goblin King. He dared not refuse for the Goblin King was very powerful. As he approached, the Goblin King was saying something. But Tassel was looking at the beauty of the Black Forest and remembering how wonderful it was the day he helped Michael, Sparkle, and a few other little people, to put the first Rainbow into the sky.

'Tassel,' said the Goblin King.

Tassel blinked his eyes and answered, 'Yes.' He did not address the Goblin King with a title for Tassel was not a goblin.

'You must take back the wishes of health, hope and happiness, which you granted to the lady for her two children.'

'I can not do that, I would be breaking my promise to the lady.'

'The children no longer believe in the fairy folk. You will take back your wishes,' insisted the Goblin King.

'I am sorry, I will not,' said Tassel softly.

The Goblin King waved his hand in the air. The other goblins in the clearing stood aside. A red bubble entered the clearing and came to rest in front of the Goblin King. The red bubble became transparent and crystal-like, and Tassel felt a chill in the air.

'Tassel,' said the Goblin King, 'you will for all time be imprisoned in this glass globe.'

Tassel felt very cold and there was a buzzing noise in his head.

'Why am I so cold? It's midsummer,' he said. A moment passed and Tassel turned into snow.

The Goblin King spoke again. 'You will lose your health, because you will be forever cold. You will lose all hope, because there will be no escape, and you will lose your happiness because you will remember what you once were.'

The Goblin King waved his arm and a door appeared in the glass globe. Tassel was pushed inside and the door vanished, and then it began to snow. The spell was cast and the deed was done. Tassel had become a Snowman, imprisoned in a glass globe where everything was white and it snowed most of the time. He tried to move but he couldn't. He was so cold and so lonely in his snow covered world.

The glass globe with its snow scene was left in the clearing and remained there for some time, until, by chance, a little boy found it and took it home.

Chapter Three

Timothy was at last sleeping soundly in his bed. He had been very busy all day and it had been a very hot summer day. He had swum across a great river and been a cowboy in the Wild West. He had tramped through the Black Forest and found a Snowman in a glass globe. Between washing in the bathroom and arriving in bed, he had climbed one of the world's highest mountains, which had been the staircase.

Yes, it had been very busy, and hot, all day. Now at last, Timothy was asleep. But before he went to sleep he placed the glass globe with its beautiful snow scene on his bedside table. Darkness filled the bedroom and a stillness fell over the house. It was midsummer and this night was midsummer night, a magic night.

The sound that awoke Timothy was the lid of the red soldiers' box falling to the floor. He sat up in bed and watched in amazement as one after the other, the soldiers climbed from their box and formed neat lines on the bedroom floor. Timothy's toy cannon was pushed into place and without warning it was fired. The cannonball made a hole in a box that was on the floor a little way from Timothy's bed. The blue soldiers that were inside, climbed out through the hole and began to form neat lines just the same as the red ones.

Timothy watched as one of the little men shouted 'FIRE!' All the rifles held by the blue soldiers flashed with light and a cracking sound filled the bedroom. The red soldiers answered with a blaze of light from their guns followed by a loud cracking sound. Soon the bedroom was filled with flashing lights and noise. The toy cannon was fired again and again until a stray shot bounced off the wardrobe and smashed the glass globe that kept the Snowman in his snow covered world. The snow drifted from the broken glass globe and landed upon the bedside table. The Snowman cried for help as the warm night air filled what was left of the broken glass globe. Timothy watched sadly as the Snowman began to melt.

Just then a breeze from the open window blew the curtains apart, and a moonbeam shone through the window settling on the floor between the rows of red and blue soldiers, who were still shooting at each other. The curtains were still fluttering in the breeze allowing moonbeams to pass between them, bringing moonlight in to the bedroom. Slowly the image of a small figure began to take shape.

Timothy could see the little figure clearly and so could the red and blue soldiers. The toy men stopped shooting at each other and silence fell upon the bedroom. They knew the figure was a fairy and they all watched the tiny figure as she flew from the floor to the bedside table. She examined the broken glass globe and the Snowman, then she turned to look at Timothy.

'Who are you?' he asked.

'I am a Moon Fairy,' she answered softly.

The Snowman was bending in the middle, and his red hat was slipping over his head, as he melted.

'Can you help him?' asked Timothy.

'Yes, I can,' she said.

'Then will you?' he asked.

'I will,' answered the Moon Fairy. She reached into the broken glass globe and touched the Snowman's arm. As soon as she touched him she knew he was one of the fairy folk.

'Timothy, I will take you and the Snowman to a magical place. When everything has been put right, I will bring you both back.'

The Moon Fairy was small although she could adjust her height when she found it necessary. She was dressed in a luminous light green flowing gown with a very pale blue cloak and hood. On her feet she wore dainty crystal clear slippers, and about her waist was a pale yellow ribbon. Her hair was shoulder length and her eyes were gold in colour.

'Come with us, Timothy,' she said.

The bedroom was filled with moonlight and slowly the wardrobe and bedside table disappeared. They were replaced by damp green grass. Timothy looked around him in amazement. The bedroom had gone and he was at a magical place with the Moon Fairy, and the Snowman.

'You are the first little boy to come to this place,' the Moon Fairy said softly.

Timothy looked around him, his eyes wide and his mouth open. The grass he was sitting on was damp from the spray from a waterfall. The sky above him was blue and the sun shone through the trees in patches of yellow. The sunlight reflected through the spray of the waterfall, forming hundreds of tiny rainbows.

'They are all magical,' said the Moon Fairy.

The Snowman stood on the soft green grass as straight and round as the Goblin King had made him. His hat fitted him perfectly and his face held a smile, the like of which Timothy had never seen before.

'Listen to the waterfall, hear the sound of fairy pipes, see the magical rainbows, and between them, see the sparkle of tiny fairy wings,' whispered the Moon Fairy.

Timothy looked, and listened, and enjoyed this place of wonder. A place so tranquil, so beautiful, so magical.

'Now is the time to tell me everything,' whispered the Moon Fairy, 'Now, while Timothy is occupied.'

The Snowman spoke. 'My name is Tassel. I am an elf. I have been turned into a Snowman by the Goblin King and imprisoned in a glass globe.'

'But you are not a goblin. He should not have done this to you,' said the Moon Fairy.

'It happened so fast, and once I was changed into a Snowman, my magic stopped working,' said Tassel.

'I promise to put everything right,' said the Moon Fairy. 'Now it is time to go.'

As the magical place slowly vanished, the Snowman spoke once more.

'Moon Fairy,' he called, 'you will find help with my friends, Michael the leprechaun, and Sparkle, the fairy of the Silver Stream. You will find them in the Black Forest.'

'I will find Michael and Sparkle, help will come to you Tassel,' she said.

The magical place was gone and as Timothy opened his eyes, the morning sun sent gentle beams of light through the slightly parted curtains into his bedroom. He looked around, hardly believing where he had been. There was no trace of the Moon Fairy, and everything looked as it had been before he went to sleep. The blue soldiers were in their box and the red ones were in theirs, but there was a hole in the blue soldiers' box that had not been there before. The Snowman was still inside the glass globe and there was no sign that it had been broken, but the Snowman, yes, the Snowman was smiling. For now he had hope.

'It did happen,' said Timothy, 'It did!'

He leapt out of bed. 'I will find the magical place again!' he said. But he never did.

The Moon Fairy shows herself once in a lifetime, and only on a midsummer night.

Chapter Four

Michael and Sparkle were making their way home through the Black Forest after a busy hot summer's day. It was beginning to get dark when Michael and Sparkle walked into a clearing near the Silver Stream. They had seen Tassel's boat stuck on the bank of the Silver Stream and expected to see him nearby. Instead amidst a cluster of moonbeams they saw something shining. It was the Moon Fairy. They walked further into the clearing, which was now filled with moonlight.

Sparkle greeted the Moon Fairy and she replied, 'I have come to tell you about your friend Tassel. He needs your help. He is trapped in a world of snow. His shape has been changed so that he can survive in his glass prison. Ride on a moonbeam, it knows where he is, help your friend. When you have found him, bring him here.'

The Moon Fairy began to vanish before their eyes. 'I must visit the Goblin King.' Her words lingered in the night air, then she was gone.

Michael and Sparkle were engulfed in moonlight and transported on a moonbeam through the night sky. They floated through the open window of Timothy's bedroom and landed at the bottom of Timothy's bed. They stepped off the moonbeam and looked around the room. The soldiers were packed away in their boxes. There was a rubber ball on the floor near the bed. In the corner of the bedroom there was a jack-in-a-box which was open, but the jack was fast asleep. On the bed lay a teddy bear with only one eye, it was half open and Michael and Sparkle were not sure if he was asleep or not. On the bedside table was a glass globe with a Snowman in it.

'There he is,' said Sparkle.

'It doesn't look like Tassel,' said Michael.

They moved to the bedside table and Michael tapped on the glass globe, but there was no response from the Snowman.

'That is Tassel,' said Sparkle. 'We must get him back to the Black Forest.'

So while Timothy slept, Sparkle waved her hand above her head and the glass globe rose slowly into the air. The moonbeam that Michael and Sparkle had travelled on moved beneath it. It was such a beautiful sight to see the moonbeam shining through the glass globe, making a strange blue light reflect through the snow covered world of the Snowman.

'Come on Michael, we haven't much time,' whispered Sparkle.

The two little people stepped onto the moonbeam and left the way they came, taking the glass globe with them. The night air was warm and the moonbeam carried them back to the clearing, near the Silver Stream in the Black Forest. They landed softly on the grass.

'We must break the glass dome and get him out,' said Sparkle.

Michael picked up a large pebble and hit the glass dome with it. The glass cracked and then the globe broke into pieces, for a moment snow flew in all directions. When it had settled the Snowman fell from the broken globe, his protection from the worm night air was gone. He lay on the soft grass and began to melt in the warmth of the summer night.

'Sparkle, isn't there anything we can do?' asked Michael.

'No,' Sparkle said sadly, as she watched the Snowman melting.

'Only the Goblin King can break the spell. If the Moon Fairy can't make him change his mind, we will lose Tassel forever.'

Chapter Five

It was dark when the Moon Fairy arrived at the goblin's caves. They were situated at the west side of the Black Forest, the other side of the Great Meadow, which was like a maze. She entered and travelled along in the dark passage. The only light was coming from the moonbeam that she was riding on.

At last the passageway opened into a cavern and in the centre, seated at a big table surrounded by other goblins, was the Goblin King. They were all eating, drinking and talking in the twilight of the cavern.

The Moon Fairy stepped from the moonbeam and increased her size until she was as tall as the Goblin King himself. She was soon noticed by the goblins and silence fell over the cavern. The Goblin King looked at her. He was a bit bigger than the other goblins. He was rounder with a fuller face. He had a more pointed nose and longer fingers with claw like fingernails. He was dressed in a dark red suit with small golden balls on his shoulders, around his middle he had a very large black buckled belt, and a gold pocket watch hung around his neck. He had found it in the Great Meadow some time ago. It wasn't working then, and it wasn't working now.

'What do you want?' he asked gruffly.

'You have imprisoned an elf in a world of everlasting snow and cold. You must set him free,' answered the Moon Fairy.

'He has granted three wishes to two children who don't believe in fairy folk,' said the Goblin King.

'How did you know about Tassel, and the three wishes?' asked the Moon Fairy.

'I know everything that happens in and around the Black Forest,' he answered.

'Tassel granted the wishes to the children's mother because she helped him. He promised the lady he would grant the wishes and he won't break his promise,' the Moon Fairy explained.

'Tassel is an elf, not a goblin. It is not for you to punish him.'

'He will be a Snowman for evermore,' said the Goblin King. 'He will stay in his snow-covered world, there will be no escape for him!'

'You are the Goblin King, I am just a Moon Fairy, one of just a few. I will tell you this, Goblin King: If you don't set the elf free, I will cause the ground under us to open up. We will all be swallowed up. We will all live in darkness for ever. We will all be lost in the tunnels under the ground. We will never see the light of the day or walk through the Black Forest again.'

The goblins began talking amongst themselves.

'Your Kingship,' said a goblin voice, 'let the Snowman go.'

Then other voices joined in, 'Yes, your Kingship. Break the spell and let the Snowman go.'

The Goblin King stood up. 'Silence!' he bellowed.

A quietness fell over the cavern.

The Goblin King spoke. 'You will be lost with us,' he said, pointing at the Moon Fairy.

'Yes, I shall,' she said, 'Forever.'

'You are going to do this for one elf?' said the Goblin King his voice getting louder.

'Yes!' she said.

The Goblin King thought for a moment, and then laughed loudly. 'Then I have no choice, the spell is broken.'

'Thank you, your Kingship,' the Moon Fairy said softly. She stepped into the moonbeam and vanished from their sight.

'All that for an elf,' said the Goblin King. 'Some folk care too much.'

The Moon Fairy's voice echoed through the passageways, 'And some not enough,' and then all was quiet.

Chapter Six

When the Moon Fairy appeared in the clearing, the Snowman stopped melting.

'Can you help Tassel?' asked Sparkle.

'It is done,' answered the Moon Fairy softly.

Before their eyes, the Snowman slowly changed his shape. He was engulfed in a bright blue shimmering light. Soon the transformation was complete and Tassel lay on the soft green grass. Michael and Sparkle helped him to his feet. He thanked them and then looked across the clearing at the Moon Fairy.

'Thank you,' he said.

The Moon Fairy smiled. Tassel felt her golden eyes looking right through him. 'I was right, wasn't I?' he asked.

'Yes Tassel, you were right,' answered the Moon Fairy.

He walked to the edge of the clearing with Michael and Sparkle. Then he turned and looked at the Moon Fairy again. 'Is there anything I must do?' he asked.

The Moon Fairy began to slowly disappear, 'Just carry on as you have been. Enjoy your adventures with your friends.'

The Moon Fairy was gone. Michael, Sparkle and Tassel looked at each other. Then they heard the Moon Fairy's voice again. 'Goodbye Tassel, Michael, Sparkle, we may meet again.'

Everything was quiet, the three fairy folk had never known the Black Forest so still. The silence was broken when Tassel asked, 'Is my boat still at the bank of the Silver Stream?'

Michael and Sparkle nodded their heads.

'We will take you to it,' said Michael. 'It is only a short distance.'

They walked through the Black Forest to the Silver Stream. When they reached the little brown boat, Michael helped Tassel to push it off the bank onto the water and Tassel climbed into it. He hoisted the white sail and a gentle breeze sent the little boat on its way.

'Goodbye Tassel,' said Sparkle.

Tassel smiled and steered the boat away from the bank, pointing it downstream towards the little cottage that was his home. 'Thank you, both,' he said.

They waved to him and watched as he sailed away. Michael and Sparkle walked side by side along the bank of the Silver Stream.

'I wonder what Tassel's next adventure will be,' said Sparkle softly.

'Yes, I wonder,' repeated Michael.

5. The Ice Crystal

Chapter One

Far away, long ago, in the furthest reaches of space, even before time began, there was a comet. It had travelled through millions of galaxies, countless milky ways. But as fate or fortune determined it finally made its way towards the Earth. The comet was a very large sphere made of stone and ice, with a long tail. As the comet passed the Earth it skimmed the Earth's atmosphere and lost part of its tail, and then continued its journey to end in destruction as it crashed into the Sun.

The piece of the comet's tail that snapped off as it bounced off the Earth's atmosphere was sphere-shaped and made of ice. It continued through our atmosphere and due to the friction and heat as it passed through the air the leading edge of the sphere became faceted. The tiny piece of the comets tail looked like a small Ice Crystal as it plummeted towards the Earth. The Ice Crystal finally landed in a slow running Silver Stream in the Black Forest.

In some parts of the Silver Stream the water was very deep and very cold. There were also lots of under water passages. The one that the Ice Crystal was in carried it under the walls of the Black Castle, eventually coming to rest in one of the dungeons, where it had found its way through a large crack in the stone wall. It lay in the darkness on the freezing cold dungeon floor for many years before the Black Witch of the Black Castle found it.

There had been an incident towards the end of the last summer when an elf named Tassel had been caught in this same dungeon. He had entered the Black Castle to retrieve a bright gem-shaped colour that was part of a rainbow. When he crossed the threshold of the castle, all his magic was drained from him. Yet when he was cornered in the dungeon he drew on all the strength in him to save himself and his friends, and he was answered. That had surprised him. It had surprised the Black Witch too.

When the Black Witch threw the gem-shaped colour at Tassel with such force, he called on all the magic that he ever knew, and was answered. As the gem-shaped colour was about to strike Tassel, his shadow stood away from the stone walls, and his reflection rose from the wet floor. Because the little gem could not hit Tassel it broke into two smaller gems. One was caught by his shadow, the other was caught by his reflection. Tassel made his escape with his friends taking the two little gems with him. The eyes of his shadow and his reflection flashed gold and then they vanished like two phantoms in the darkness. It surprised the Black Witch, and that is why she didn't pursue him. She had searched the dungeon for the source of the magic and at last she found the Ice Crystal.

The Black Witch placed the Ice Crystal in a glass globe and created a snow storm around it, so that it wouldn't melt. She studied it all through the winter. The Ice Crystal sparkled in the glistening snow.

The Black Witch worked out that for each flat surface, and there were many of them, there was a different magical power. The Ice Crystal could see the past, the present, the future, things that will be, might be, or could be.

The Black Witch was gazing into the Ice Crystal, watching Tassel the little elf. She had been watching him all through the winter. Now it was springtime. She knew he was going to visit the Fairy Sea Queen, but did not know when. The Ice Crystal had many powers and the Black Witch had only discovered a few, so far.

It had been a long, cold winter, but now spring was in the air. Tassel, the little elf who lived in the cottage by the Silver Stream, was venturing out to visit the Fairy Sea Queen. It was a long way for a little elf, but he did have his little brown boat. As he left the beautiful garden that was part of the little cottage, he didn't know that he was being watched by the Black Witch through the Ice Crystal.

The Black Witch had also learned through the Ice Crystal that the Fairy Sea Queen was very powerful and that most of her power was in her crown. The Black Witch had a plan to steal the Fairy Sea Queen's crown, and so she left her Black Castle to trick Tassel into taking her with him.

The Black Witch transported herself to the grassy bank of the Silver Stream and waited for Tassel. It wasn't long before Tassel's little brown boat with its white sail came into sight. The Black Witch wove her spell and turned herself into an exact likeness of Tassel. As Tassel approached, he could not believe his eyes. Standing on the bank waving to him was... him! How could this be?

As he approached, he heard himself say, 'Hi Tassel, can I visit the Fairy Sea Queen with you?'

Tassel brought his boat to a stop close to the bank.

'Who are you?' he asked.

'I am you,' came the reply.

'When your shadow and reflection separated from you, I was created.'

This explanation seemed feasible and so Tassel accepted it. The Black Witch, in her new disguise, stepped into Tassel's boat and they continued on their way, to visit the Fairy Sea Queen.

The Black Witch was identical to Tassel in every way: blue shirt, blue trousers, a red hat with red boots and a silver belt about his waist. Even he couldn't tell the difference. Every time Tassel tried to say something, the other Tassel answered before he had time to finish what he was saying. It was most disturbing.

The voyage was quite a long one, and Tassel was very uneasy. He could understand how this situation could have occurred, but something was not right and he didn't know quite what it was.

At last, the little brown boat and its unusual crew arrived at the place where the Silver Stream joined the Sea. Tassel stepped out of the boat and with the other Tassel's help, pulled it out of the water onto the sand. As he looked up, he saw a sea sprite. He was dressed in blue from head to foot, with gold-coloured eyes. Before he had a chance to say anything, the sea sprite spoke.

'Hi, Tassel,' he said.

'Surf,' said Tassel.

Tassel wasn't sure if it was Surf, because all the sea sprites looked the same, and there were more approaching across the sandy beach. Surf looked at the two Tassels.

'What is happening?' he asked.

The answer was forthcoming as he spoke. The Black Witch returned to her rightful form.

'All of you sea sprites will obey me!' she shouted. 'All of you go to your Queen and bring me her crown!'

The sea sprites ran across the beach and entered a dark cave. Tassel followed them, and he entered the cave. It took a while for his eyes to adjust to the darkness and what he saw, he didn't like. The sea sprites had taken the Fairy Sea Queen's golden crown. They pushed past Tassel and out of the cave into the sunlight. Tassel could now see the Fairy Sea Queen and he approached slowly.

Around her was a dark velvet blue cloak. Her eyes were luminous green, her hair golden yellow. She wore a dark green blouse and matching dress, a brown waistcoat with yellow laces. At her waist was a brown belt with a gold buckle, and at her wrists were brown leather guards.

'I am sorry, Your Majesty,' Tassel said softly.

'It's not your fault, Tassel,' she said. She had known Tassel for some time as he had come to her for help a long time ago when he was covered in luminous moondust.

'The Black Witch from the Black Castle is doing this,' Tassel explained. 'She tricked me into bringing her with me. I was only coming to visit you, but I have brought you a lot of trouble. The sea sprites are being controlled by her. They did take the crown, didn't they?' he asked.

'Yes, they did,' replied the Fairy Sea Queen.

'I will get it back,' said Tassel. He turned to leave.

'Tassel,' the Fairy Sea Queen called after him. 'Take my wand. It's not as powerful as the crown, but it will help you.' Tassel thanked her, pushing the silver wand into his belt he left her in the darkness of the cave.

Tassel left the cave and found his way through the dark passages. As he emerged into the daylight, he saw the last of the sea sprites diving into the centre of a very large wave. The wave was the length of the beach and looked like a tumbling tube of water.

Tassel dived into the side of the wave without thinking of the outcome. To his amazement, he found he could fly! And so, he flew through the centre of the wave, walls of water all around him. This was new, he had never done anything like this before.

'It must be the wand,' he thought to himself. Then quite suddenly, the wave broke as it hit the beach. Tassel found himself staggering out of the water, and then falling onto the sandy beach. When he opened his eyes, Surf the sea sprite was sitting next to him. They were both very wet.

'What happened?' asked Surf.

'The sea sprites were under a spell of the Black Witch. They stole the Fairy Sea Queen's crown,' explained Tassel.

'I saw a black figure leaving the beach and entering the trees beyond,' said Surf.

'She will be going back through the Black Forest to her Black Castle. If she gets there I may not be able to retrieve the Fairy Sea Queen's crown,' explained Tassel. He dragged himself to his feet and made his way to his boat. He pushed it off the sand and into the water.

'Surf,' said Tassel.

'Will you try to look after the Fairy Sea Queen? I will try to get her crown back.'

'Is that the Fairy Sea Queen's wand in your belt?' asked Surf.

'Yes,' replied Tassel.

'It will give you five extra powers,' said Surf, 'I don't know what they will be, they are different for whoever possesses the wand.'

'I will need all the help I can get,' said Tassel, 'I will try to find some friends to help me. Goodbye, Surf. I don't know how long this is going to take.'

Surf said goodbye and watched as Tassel sailed his little brown boat up stream.

Chapter Two

The Black Witch had returned to the Black Castle and had been there for some time, gazing into the Ice Crystal. One of the facets had found Tassel. This is what the Black Witch had been waiting for.

He was standing on the bank of the Silver Stream, talking to Michael the leprechaun and Sparkle the fairy of the Silver Stream. Michael was dressed in emerald green, on his feet he wore brown leather boots and around his waist was a brown leather belt with a golden buckle. Sparkle, the fairy of the Silver Stream, was dressed in a flowing lemon-coloured gown with a white belt and a silver buckle. Her golden hair almost matched the lemon colour of her clothes. They had finished making their plans and had started their journey to the Black Castle.

The Black Witch was still staring into the Ice Crystal when she noticed in one of the other facets an even greater danger than Tassel. It was the Goblin King. Somehow he had gained knowledge of the Fairy Sea Queen's crown and he and a band of goblins were also making their way to the Black Castle. The Black Witch realised that the goblins and Tassel, with his two friends, would arrive at the same time.

The Black Witch then turned her attention to the Fairy Sea Queen's crown. She tried to make the crown fit on her head, and eventually the crown was forced into place. But, as with all things that are forced, it broke. The crown glowed brightly, and then changed to a dull gold colour. It had a big split on one side. The Black Witch felt it go, and then felt a very strange sensation. All the Fairy Sea Queen's magic was flowing from the crown, down the Black Witch's face, over her shoulder and down her long black gown onto the cold stone floor where it lay making a white puddle.

Then another strange thing happened. Where the Fairy Sea Queen's Good Magic had flowed like water down the Black Witch's side, it had left a streak of Good Magic. Now the Black Witch's magic powers were being drained from her through the streak of Good Magic, and lay on the cold stone floor making a black puddle.

The Black Witch tried to pick up her Black Magic from the black puddle but it just ran through her fingers. She tried to pick up the Good Magic from the white puddle but that did the same. It made her fingers tingle as they passed through it. She took the broken crown from her head and placed it on the table next to the Ice Crystal, which was still inside its glass globe, the snow lying dormant around it.

Then the Black Witch had an idea. She took the Ice Crystal from the glass globe and placed it on the floor between the two puddles of magic. The Ice Crystal attracted both black and white puddles of magic, and in no time at all, both magic puddles had been absorbed into the Ice Crystal. The Black Witch picked up and carefully placed the Ice Crystal back into the snow filled glass globe. She gave the globe a little shake, just enough to make the snow flutter around the Ice Crystal. The Ice Crystal had a slightly darker glint in its facets as the snow swirled around inside the glass globe. Something had happened. The Black Witch had changed. She wasn't sure in which way, but she felt different. She left the Ice Crystal in its glass globe and waited for the visitors that she knew were coming.

The Goblin King and his band of goblins had started out early from the goblin caves. It had been a long trek across the Great Meadow, that was now a maze, and through the Black Forest to the walls of the Black Castle. It was not so far for Tassel, Michael and Sparkle, the fairy of the Silver Stream, so they reached the Black Castle first.

But it was still the end of the day, darkness was falling over the Black Forest. This made the Black Castle look even more frightening. The Black Witch had seen them arrive through the Ice Crystal. She had also seen the Goblin King and his band of goblins arriving at the walls of the Black Castle.

The Black Witch didn't know why but she found herself opening the big main door and inviting Tassel and his two friends in. She closed the big door behind them.

'I know I have been bad in the past,' she said, 'but something has happened to me.'

'What is this white streak?' asked Tassel as he pointed at the white lines running from the Black Witch's head to her feet.

'I stole the Fairy Sea Queen's crown. Unfortunately, I broke it while trying to put it on. I think this is Good Magic that I have stuck to me.'

'Where is the crown?' asked Tassel.

'It is in one of the dungeons. Come with me. I will take you to it,' replied the Black Witch.

'Careful,' whispered Michael, for he knew what the Black Witch was capable of.

'I won't harm you, any of you. You see, I have changed.' said the Black Witch.

When they reached the dungeon, they saw the Fairy Sea Queen's crown. Sparkle looked around at everything very carefully. 'The Fairy Sea Queen's crown has lost all of its magical powers. I think you posses some of them in the white streaks,' she said, pointing at the Black Witch.

'Is that why I feel so different?' she asked.

'I think so,' answered Sparkle, 'Is there anything else that might have magical powers here?'

Tassel thought for a moment. 'Only this,' he said, pulling the Fairy Sea Queen's wand from his belt.

'It doesn't feel very strong,' said Sparkle.

'The Fairy Sea Queen said it could help, but I'm not sure what it can do,' Tassel replied.

The Black Witch showed the little people the Ice Crystal. As soon as Sparkle saw it, she said, 'I have seen one of these before. It is cold and powerful. Its colour takes on whatsoever is inside it. It comes from the heavens, from outer space. It absorbs magical power and I don't know what else it will have absorbed, as it travelled through the coldness of space.'

Michael looked at the Ice Crystal. 'It is mostly crystal clear, except for some white cloud with dark edges,' he said.

'It looks like a thunder cloud,' added Tassel.

'The Fairy Sea Queen's magic has mixed with the Black Witch's magic, and that is why the Ice Crystal has a thunder cloud in it,' explained Sparkle. 'The Ice Crystal is a very dangerous thing, and we don't know how to control it.'

Then, in one of the facets, they saw the Goblin King and his band of goblins climbing over the castle wall.

'They are in the Castle! What do they want?' Michael asked with alarm.

The Black Witch answered, 'They knew I was going to steal the Fairy Sea Queen's crown. I think the Goblin King is going to steal it from me.'

'But it's drained of all its magic,' said Sparkle.

'He doesn't know I broke it,' said the Black Witch.

The Goblin King and his goblins were now running through the dark passages of the Black Castle, upstairs and downstairs, in and out of stone rooms, through the dimly lit corridors. At last they came running into the dungeon where the Black Witch and the three little people were standing.

The Goblin King saw the Fairy Sea Queen's crown. He grabbed it, and pushed it firmly onto his head.

The crown glowed for a second or two, and then went back to a dull gold colour. A second crack appeared in the crown and it fell to the floor, breaking into two pieces. The Ice Crystal glowed as it absorbed the last of the power from the Fairy Sea Queen's crown.

'MINE!' shouted the Goblin King, as he snatched the two pieces of broken crown.

'The crown belongs to the Fairy Sea Queen,' said Tassel.

'Not any more,' snarled the Goblin King as he and his band of goblins left the dungeon. 'I will have the crown repaired, and then everyone from the Sandy Beach to the Great Meadow will bow...TO ME!'

'I don't think so,' whispered Sparkle as she opened the glass globe that was keeping the Ice Crystal cold. All the colours of the spectrum rose from its facets and engulfed the dungeon. They flowed through the passageways up the stone steps into every room. The colours were everywhere. They breezed around the little people and engulfed the goblin King and his band of goblins. The Black Castle was wrapped in rainbow colours, so bright, so powerful that the Goblin King and his band of goblins ran out of the Black Castle, and kept on running until they reached the maze that was the Great Meadow. The Black Witch, Michael, Sparkle and Tassel managed to get outside before the great transformation started.

The Black Castle disappeared from view and, where it had been, there seemed to be a large pillar of light that rose into the air, up, up and up until at the top it spread out like a mushroom, and all the colours of the spectrum rained down on the Black Forest.

'I think everything is about to change,' said Sparkle.

When all the colours had finally stopped raining down, the Black Castle had gone. In its place stood a little Woodland Cottage and standing outside it was a little old lady with grey hair.

The Black Witch was nowhere to be found. The three little people just looked in amazement.

'Can she see us?' asked Michael.

'I don't think so,' replied Sparkle.

Then something even more amazing happened. All the colours that had tumbled down on them all rushed together. They were drawn to the Ice Crystal, and entered it. Sparkle was still holding the glass globe and watched as the spectrum of light passed into it, and sealed it as it did. She did not know what made her say what she did. 'Thanks to the Ice Crystal, the Black Castle is now a Woodland Cottage, and the Black Forest is now the Green Woodland. The maze will have become the Great Meadow again.' She thought for a moment and then added. 'I think I have lost my magical powers.'

Michael tried to vanish, and then he said, 'I have lost mine too and someone has found my crock of gold.'

They both looked at Tassel. 'Mine have gone, but there may be something left in the Fairy Sea Queen's wand. But I don't really know.'

The old lady with grey hair turned and went back into the Woodland Cottage. She had a sense of peace about her, even the little people could sense it.

Tassel said, 'I can't take the Fairy Sea Queen's crown back to her, but we could take the Ice Crystal.'

Michael and Sparkle thought for a moment, then Michael said, 'We don't know what to do with it, do we?'

'No,' said Tassel and Sparkle together.

'The Fairy Sea Queen is very wise,' added Tassel.

'She may be able to help us get our magical powers back,' said Sparkle.

'But she has no magical powers at all! She gave all she had to me in the wand,' explained Tassel.

'Then we must take the Ice Crystal to her,' said Michael.

So it was decided that they would journey to the end of the Sparkling Silver Stream, for now the Silver Stream was sparkling again.

Chapter Three

While they walked through the ever-changing forest they tried to understand what had happened. Due to the great transformation and all the bright lights and colours, the night had passed almost without being noticed. The Black Forest had settled into being the Green Woodland and everything felt as it should. When they reached the Sparkling Silver Stream they did not stop, they boarded Tassel's little brown boat and they set sail downstream to the sea and the caves, where the Fairy Sea Queen lived. It was midday when they reached the end of the Sparkling Silver Stream.

Waiting for them was a figure Tassel had met before. It was Surf the sea sprite. Tassel introduced Surf to Michael and Sparkle. Surf's golden eyes opened wide and he said, 'I have heard a lot of stories of the fairy of the Sparkling Silver Stream and, now, here you are!'

The smile on Surf's face vanished when he heard what had happened. He led the way to the Fairy Sea Queen's cave. When they reached the entrance, he stopped, 'I should wait here,' Surf said, 'She hasn't seen anyone since her crown was taken.'

'But we must see her,' said Tassel.

He entered the cave, Michael and Sparkle followed him. He walked through the passageways as if he knew them.

'Wait for us,' called Michael.

'Sorry!' said Tassel, 'I can see through the darkness, it must be the Fairy Sea Queen's magic wand,' he added.

It was not long before the three little people found themselves in a large cavern.

'This is where I saw her last,' said Tassel looking all around him.

'Your Majesty,' said Sparkle softly, 'will you come and talk to us?'

'I do not have any magical powers,' came the reply from the darkness.

'Perhaps we can help each other,' Sparkle said as she placed the glass globe with the Ice Crystal in it, gently on the cavern floor. From out of the shadows stepped the Fairy Sea Queen. She moved to the centre of the cavern.

'I cannot help you,' she said.

The Fairy Sea Queen approached slowly, never taking her eyes from the glass globe and the shining object within. 'It is an Ice Crystal,' she said. 'Why are there grey and black flashes in it?'

She answered her own question. 'It has been in contact with dark, no, Black Magic. The clear parts of the crystal must be Good Magic. I have seen an Ice Crystal before, only one, this is the second. But this one is not right.'

Sparkle tried to explain, 'We were in the Black Castle, in the Black Forest, and while we were trying to get your crown back, we were exposed to the Ice Crystal's power.'

'Was the Black Witch there?' asked the Fairy Sea Queen.

'Yes, and the Goblin King, and some of his goblin band.' answered Michael.

'The Black Witch broke your crown, it wouldn't fit on her head,' said Tassel. 'That's why it broke. The Goblin King knew the Black Witch had stolen your crown. He knows most things that happen in and around the Green Woodland. He had come to steal it from the Black Witch, but she broke it first. He took it away, and went back across the Great Meadow to the goblin caves. I am sorry I failed to get your crown back. We lost all our magical powers when we were exposed to the Ice Crystal. All the magic that is left is in your magic wand,' explained Tassel.

The Fairy Sea Queen picked up the glass globe and looked at the Ice Crystal carefully. Then she said, 'May I have the wand?'

Tassel took it from his belt and gave it to her. They watched as the Fairy Sea Queen touched the glass globe with the wand. The wand changed from silver to gold and glowed brightly. The Fairy Sea Queen picked up an open shell from the cavern floor and set the wand between the shell and the glass globe. The darker colours, grey and black left the Ice Crystal, flowing through the wand and landed in the sea shell. After a while the Ice Crystal was sparkling and clear.

The Fairy Sea Queen's wand remained bright gold. The shell that the darkened colours were drained into was carefully placed inside a tiny Treasure Chest. The lid was closed and the Fairy Sea Queen locked it. The three little people watched as the key vanished from their sight.

'Where is the key?' asked Tassel.

'Only I know where it is. This is how it must be,' answered the Fairy Sea Queen, 'This must never be opened,' she added.

She picked up the Treasure Chest of Magic and took it to the back of the cavern where she placed it in the rock pool. She watched as it sank until it was out of sight.

'No one will be able to retrieve it from the depths of the rock pool, even I don't know how deep it is,' said the Fairy Sea Queen.

'Is the Treasure Chest of Magic gone forever?' asked Tassel.

'Yes, it is,' replied the Fairy Sea Queen.

The Fairy Sea Queen's wand was still touching the glass globe and, as she picked it up, she said something that the three little people didn't quite hear, and the wand changed into a golden sword. The Fairy Sea Queen turned to the three little people and said, 'Tassel, will you try again to bring my crown to me?'

'Yes, I will try,' he answered.

She looked at Sparkle and Michael, 'Will you try to help him?' she asked.

'Yes,' Michael and Sparkle answered together.

The Fairy Sea Queen went on as she gave the golden sword to Tassel. 'All you have is the magic in the sword. As I come to understand the Ice Crystal, I will try to return your magical powers to you. If I am successful, they may not be as they were.'

'Thank you for trying,' said Sparkle.

The little people turned and left the cavern. They wound their way through the tunnels and at last out into the sunshine and sand. Surf was waiting for them. Tassel told him what had happened while they were in the caves with the Fairy Sea Queen. Surf saw them safely to Tassel's little boat and waved goodbye as they set off back upstream.

By the time they reached Sparkle's under water Magical Cave, they were very tired. It had been two days and a night since Tassel started his adventure but they were now at Sparkle's Magical Cave and, since they had all lost their magical powers, they all had to climb into the Magical Cave through the little hole in the top that was hidden between the roots of a willow tree.

It was quite a dangerous climb and only fairy folk could pass through the entrance to the cave, but they all eventually arrived safely inside. Sparkle soon made something nice to eat, and the three little people talked about their adventures.

In a little while, they fell asleep, Sparkle in her little bed, Michael and Tassel on the floor. Sparkle's Cave really was a magical place. The walls were solid rock and the cave was spherical in shape, but one side of the cave was all water, it was pure magic that kept the water out. Sparkle often used the water wall to enter and leave the cave. This is why she was called the Fairy of the Sparkling Silver Stream.

There were two little chairs and a table. The only other object in the Magical Cave was a mirror. It made the cave look much bigger than it was. This was the mirror Sparkle once used to send a Rainbow into the sky some time ago.

Chapter Four

They slept long and deep. Sparkle was the first to awaken. The morning sun was shining through the Sparkling Silver Stream and into the Magical underwater Cave. Michael and Tassel soon awoke and looked at the sunshine.

'Nice to see the sun,' said Tassel.

Michael touched the wall of water with his finger. 'What is holding it back?' he asked.

'This is a magical place, the cave has it's own magic. That is why the Sparkling Silver Stream never enters. This is why I live here,' answered Sparkle.

Michael waved his hand in the air and expected to vanish, but he was still there. 'That is not right,' he said.

Tassel took the sword from his belt and waved it in the air, nothing happened. He did look very surprised.

'This doesn't work either,' he said.

'It will when you need it,' said Sparkle with a smile.

'Hope so,' answered Tassel.

It was a new day, and the sun felt warm to them as they climbed out of Sparkle's Magical Cave. The Sparkling Silver Stream babbled past as it had done for hundreds of years.

The three little people started their journey through the Green Woodland that had been the Black Forest for so long. They walked and walked for a long time, talking about all kinds of things but mostly about how they had lost their magical powers and how they could try to get them back.

It wasn't too long before they arrived at the site where the Black Castle once stood. The little Woodland Cottage was still there, and the grey-haired old lady was still there too

'Strange to think she was the Black Witch,' said Michael.

'Once we face the Goblin King, I think a lot of things are going to change,' said Tassel.

They proceeded with their journey until they came to the edge of the Green Woodland and started to venture across the Great Meadow. This was the place where the wood nymphs lived but not one had been seen since the Green Woodland had been changed into the Black Forest and the Great Meadow into a maze. It was different now. The Great Meadow seemed a warmer friendlier place.

'Come on,' said Tassel as he led the way into the long grass.

Michael, Sparkle and Tassel did not know it at the time, but the wood nymphs saw them arrive at the Great Meadow. They also knew who they were and of the great deeds they had been responsible for, from the Great Meadow to the end of the Sparkling Silver Stream.

They watched over them as they crossed the Great Meadow ensuring that no harm came to them and soon the three little people emerged from the Great Meadow. As soon as they stepped out of the long grass they could see the goblin caves. It had been a long journey and they were very tired.

Tassel wanted to go on and confront the Goblin King and get back what was left of the Fairy Sea Queen's crown. Michael and Sparkle wanted to wait but went with Tassel to the entrance of the goblin caves. Darkness was beginning to fall as they were coming to the end of another day. This was a time when shadows grew bigger, when Dark Magic was stronger than Good Magic, when good was not always triumphant.

'We will do anything we can to help you, Tassel,' said Sparkle, 'but we have no magic to offer you.'

'Wait for me here,' said Tassel. He turned and walked into the darkness of the goblin caves. Deeper and deeper he went, until he arrived at the main cavern.

The Goblin King was in the process of pouring what looked like liquid gold into a casting. 'If I can't wear it as a crown, it will become my magical sword,' he said. He poured wine over the casting to cool it down. Then he picked up the sword and waved it in the air. It left a blue trail behind it as he waved it around his head.

'If I have any chance at all I must try to take the sword now, before he learns how to use it,' Tassel thought to himself. Tassel was no match for the Goblin King, as he was much bigger than Tassel.

'It's now or never,' thought Tassel.

He drew the sword that the Fairy Sea Queen had made for him from her magic wand, and boldly marched into the cavern. On seeing him the goblins stopped talking, and a silence fell upon the cavern.

'You!' said the Goblin King, 'You dare to enter my caves?'

'I have come to take back the Fairy Sea Queen's crown,' said Tassel in a loud voice.

'It is no longer a crown,' said the Goblin King, still waving the golden sword around.

'I wish you were more my size,' said Tassel.

To his amazement the Goblin King shrank to the same size as Tassel! The Goblin King didn't know that Tassel's sword had been the Fairy Sea Queen's magic wand.

The Goblin King tried to hit Tassel with his sword but Tassel blocked each blow. As the two swords struck each other, there were lots of blue and gold sparks and flashing light. Then Tassel realised he didn't have to fight the Goblin King, he just had to use the wishes in the sword for, after all, it was a magic wand too.

'I wish you were smaller than me,' said Tassel.

The Goblin King shrank to half Tassel's size. The sword he was holding became too heavy for him and it fell to the floor of the cavern. Tassel picked it up and, with a sword in each hand, he shouted, 'Don't any of you follow me, or you will be as small as your king.'

He left the cavern and ran through the tunnels until he found himself outside in the night air with Michael and Sparkle. He showed them the two swords and they left the goblin caves and started to cross the Great Meadow.

It was very dark, and soon they wondered if they were walking in the right direction. Then Tassel saw a tiny light, and another, and another. Then Michael and Sparkle could see them too.

'It's the wood nymphs!' said Michael.

'That's a good sign,' said Sparkle. 'They haven't been here since the Green Woodland became the Black Forest.'

Everyone knew of the wood nymphs and their tiny lights that guided lost travellers to safety. The little lights guided Michael, Sparkle and Tassel to the edge of the Great Meadow, and then they were gone.

'Thank you!' called Sparkle.

'Good to know you are back in the Great Meadow again,' added Michael.

'We never left,' came the answer on a gentle breeze.

'I wonder where they have been,' asked Michael.

'That would be a story I would like to hear one day,' said Tassel.

Now that they were back in the Green Woodland, they moved quite quickly. They were pleased to see that the Woodland Cottage was still there and not the Black Castle that had frightened everyone for so long. It wasn't long before they reached the Sparkling Silver Stream and Sparkle's Magical cave. Tassel's boat was still tied to the reeds at the bank.

'It is nearly morning. Shall we keep going and return these swords to the Fairy Sea Queen?' asked Tassel.

'I think we should,' answered Michael.

So they untied the boat and sailed on. The journey was quiet and uneventful until they reached the sea. Tassel didn't know how he did it but they were met by Surf the sea sprite.

'Hello!' he called, 'the Fairy Sea Queen is waiting for you.'

'How did she know we were coming?' asked Michael.

'She knows everything,' replied Surf.

It was now mid-morning, the yellow sunlight made everyone and everything feel good again. When they reached the Fairy Sea Queen's cave, Surf stopped quite abruptly.

'I will wait here,' he said.

The three little people entered the cave and followed the dark tunnel until it opened into the cavern where the Fairy Sea Queen was waiting for them. At the back of the cavern the Ice Crystal twinkled inside the glass globe. Tassel handed both golden swords to the Fairy Sea Queen.

'This one was your crown, and this one was your wand,' he said.

'I see that some of the magic from the wand has passed into the sword the Goblin King made,' she said.

'That must have been the blue flashes I saw,' said Tassel.

The Fairy Sea Queen placed both swords next to the Ice Crystal.

'Watch,' she said.

The two swords began to melt into a pool of golden glittering gold. It shone, fusing into the purest fairy gold ever to be seen by fairy folk. Then it shaped itself into a golden crown. The Fairy Sea Queen started to pick it up but the bottom rim of the crown broke away and fell to the ground. As it landed the rim broke and formed a Golden Belt, with a Golden Buckle at one end. The Fairy Sea Queen placed the golden crown on her head. The cave filled with light and the Ice Crystal broke free from the glass globe and formed a pillar of white light. It moved across the cavern and through the passageways until it was outside the caves. The Fairy Sea Queen and the three little people watched as the blur of light moved across the sand and out to sea.

'It is free. It is leaving us,' said the Fairy Sea Queen.

'Is it alive?' asked Sparkle.

'I don't think so,' answered the Fairy Sea Queen.

They watched as the pillar of light rose from the sea and into the sky. They watched until they couldn't see it any more. Not even the

Fairy Sea Queen knew that the Ice Crystal had to return to the coldness of space, in search of the comet, that had brought it to the little people. They could never know that the Ice Crystal would never find it.

Sparkle turned to the Fairy Sea Queen and said softly, 'I think it is time we went home.'

'Yes, I think it is,' added Michael.

'Just before you go, Tassel, I have something for you,' said the Fairy Sea Queen. Tassel turned and stood before the Fairy Sea Queen.

'Tassel, this is for you.' She handed Tassel a Golden Belt.

'Thank you, Your Majesty,' he said as he took off his silver belt and replaced it with the golden one. Then suddenly he felt a force, the like of which he had never felt before. He looked at the Fairy Sea Queen. He couldn't find the words, so the Fairy Sea Queen spoke instead. 'I know, its power is almost unlimited and the magic will be with you as long as you are wearing it.'

Tassel looked at Michael and Sparkle, and then at the Fairy Sea Queen.

'No,' said the Fairy Sea Queen, 'they do not have their magical powers back, only you. And the magic you have is not in you, it's in the Magical Golden Belt.'

Tassel started to ask a question, but the Fairy Sea Queen interrupted him.

'Can I?' he started to say.

'Of course you can,' she said, 'and you can make them more powerful than they were.'

'Thank you, Your Majesty. Can I give them their magical powers now?' he asked.

'Try your own magic first, and then when you can control what you have, give to Michael and Sparkle their magic,' she answered.

The three little people said goodbye and started to walk across the sand to where Tassel's boat was. Then the Fairy Sea Queen called to Tassel. 'Tassel, you are always welcome.'

'Thank you, Your Majesty,' he called back, but when he looked, she had gone.

Chapter Five

Surf the sea sprite had appeared and was walking with them to Tassel's little brown boat. Once they were aboard, Tassel hoisted the white sail. Surf said goodbye and the little boat started its journey back upstream. Somehow the Sparkling Silver Stream seemed brighter than it had been. The Green Woodland was greener, the sky was bluer and the sun shone brighter. Tassel turned to his two friends and said, 'Michael and Sparkle, all your magical powers will return as from this moment. Michael, we will find your crock of gold, with its three wishes, and you will have all the trickery that you had before. Sparkle, you will be as wise and beautiful as ever, and you will both be guardians of the Green Woodland, as you were before.' Michael asked, 'Are my powers restored now?'

'I think they should be,' answered Tassel.

Michael waved his hand in the air, and he vanished. A moment or two passed and he reappeared. 'Thank you Tassel,' he said, 'That works very well.'

The little brown boat sailed on upstream and, as they entered the Green Woodland, everything was at peace. Life had been restored to how things once were. It was a beautiful sunny day and all was well. When they reached Sparkle's Magical Cave, Tassel tied his boat to some reeds and left his two friends. He walked on through the Green Woodland, past the Woodland Cottage and into the Great Meadow where the wood nymphs guided him to the middle.

As he approached the centre of the Great Meadow, the Great Wizard appeared. His black and gold cloak wrapped around him. He greeted Tassel and said. 'Well done, Tassel! All is as it should be again, thanks to you and your friends. Tassel, can I ask you to be the Guardian of the Great Meadow and the Green Woodland?'

'Yes, I will do my best to keep it safe,' replied Tassel.

'One other thing,' said the Great Wizard, 'I can give you all the powers of a Wizard. You could even become a Wizard.'

Tassel smiled and said, 'I would just like to live in the Green Woodland with my friends.'

'Very well,' said the Great Wizard. 'You will have great magical power, more than you know. Use it when you need it.'

'Can I ask, Great Wizard, have you been watching us all through this dark time?'

The Great Wizard answered, 'A wizard can be many things, a shadow, a reflection, a sea sprite or even a Moon Fairy.'

Tassel smiled. The Wizard vanished from his sight. Tassel called, 'Thank you!' after him, but there was no answer. Tassel wandered back across the Great Meadow, seeing two or three wood nymphs on his way. Then he entered the Green Woodland.

It was so good to see the Sparkling Silver Stream sparkling in the sunlight again, and the Green Woodland never seemed more magical to him. He touched the Magical Golden Belt that was around his waist, and vanished. Nothing felt more right.

In his invisible state, he touched the Magical Golden Belt again and this time, flew into the sky. He looked down on the Green Woodland and the Great Meadow. The Sparkling Silver Stream never looked brighter. All was peaceful.

Then Tassel had an idea. He turned in the air and flew back across the Great Meadow and landed outside the goblin caves. He touched the Magical Golden Belt and became visible again. Then he walked into the goblin caves. It was very dark, but Tassel could see very well. It wasn't long before he reached the main cavern.

The Goblin King was shouting at the goblins, but they were not listening to him. Then one of the goblins noticed Tassel standing in the middle of the main entrance to the cavern.

'Hey!' he shouted, 'the elf is back!'

The other goblins turned to look at Tassel. The Goblin King rose from his throne and boldly walked towards Tassel. The other goblins stood aside and let their king through. 'Why are you here?' asked the Goblin King.

'I have come to return you to your rightful size,' replied Tassel.

'And just how do you think you can do that?' enquired the Goblin King.

Tassel touched the Magical Golden Belt. 'By wishing it,' he said.

The Goblin King began to grow. His black boots turned brown, his shirt and trousers turned a dark green, his ears became a little more pointed than they had been, and his face wore a smile.

'Sorry about the smile,' said Tassel.

'What have you done?' asked the Goblin King.

'You are still the Goblin King,' said Tassel, 'but I have turned you into a hobgoblin. You will be nicer than you were before, and a little taller. You will dress mainly in dark green and treat other fairy folk fairly. You will, however, have a good sense of humour. You will like yourself more, and so will others. Of course, there will be the silly tricks you will play on everyone, but that is what a hobgoblin does, even if he is a king.'

The Hobgoblin King didn't know what to say or what to do.

'I shall be watching you,' said Tassel.

Then he touched his Magical Golden Belt and vanished. He made his way back through the dark passageway and out of the goblin caves. As soon as he was out he touched his Magical Golden Belt again and flew into the sky. It wasn't long before the Green Woodland and the Sparkling Silver Stream came into sight. Then Tassel heard a voice in his head. 'Well done, Tassel, I would have done the same.'

Tassel smiled a smile that only his closest friends had ever seen. 'Will you be watching?' he asked. There was no answer, and Tassel didn't really expect one.

He flew down to follow the Sparkling Silver Stream, and it wasn't long before he arrived at Sparkle's underwater Magical cave. He landed softly on the bank of the Sparkling Silver Stream and, as he did, he touched his Magical Golden Belt and became visible again.

Michael and Sparkle came to greet him. The three little people sat on the soft green grassy bank of the Sparkling Silver Stream.

Tassel's little brown boat was still tied to the reeds, bobbing up and down on the water. It was a beautiful day. At last everything is at peace and all is well.

6. The Stolen Stream

Chapter One

In a place not far from here, there stands the Great Meadow. It is bathed in sunshine, covered with soft green grass, and sprinkled with white daisies, yellow buttercups and dandelions, with patches of purple clover. The Great Meadow is home to lots of wood nymphs and, while the buttercups and daisies give colour to the Great Meadow during the day, the lights from the lanterns of the wood nymphs make it beautiful to look at in the darkness of the night. It is said that the Great Wizard lives in the Great Meadow, but is not often seen.

To one side of the Great Meadow, there is a hill and, at the bottom of it, there is a cave. Inside the cave there are lots of passageways and in the main cavern lived a band of goblins. They are led by their King, who is a hobgoblin. He is bigger than the rest of the band. He was the one who thought of most of their plans, and was troublesome to other fairy folk.

At the other side of the Great Meadow is the Green Woodland. It is a beautiful place with a little Woodland Cottage wherein lived a little old lady with grey hair. She loved to look after her garden which had many colourful flowers.

A little further into the Green Woodland is the Sparkling Silver Stream. It brings beauty and life to the Green Woodland. It flows from the furthest point of the Green Woodland right down to the sea. About half way through the Green Woodland, the Sparkling Silver Stream passes a very magical place. It is an underwater cave and in this cave lives Sparkle, the fairy of the Sparkling Silver Stream. There is an entrance to Sparkle's cave on the bank of the Sparkling Silver Stream, but it is very well hidden between the roots of a very big willow tree. The other entrance is underwater and the cave being a very magical place, never lets the water in, though Sparkle would use it to enter and leave her cave seemingly without getting wet. This is why she was called the fairy of the Sparkling Silver Stream.

Somewhere around the area of the underwater cave, also lives a leprechaun. His name is Michael. He never told anyone where he lived, but it was somewhere near. He also had a crock of gold, but he never spoke much about it.

If we follow the Sparkling Silver Stream on its way to the sea, it passes a little cottage with a big garden. This is no ordinary little cottage, for in it lives an elf. People also live in the cottage, but the elf, who's name is Tassel, tries not to show himself to them. Tassel is a very special elf, for he has the magical powers of a Wizard that were given to him by the Great Wizard some time ago. He also has a Magical Golden Belt that was given to him by the Fairy Sea Queen.

Today, Tassel was dressed in a blue shirt and trousers, red boots with a matching red hat. About his waist was the Magical Golden Belt.

This morning Tassel had walked through the little cottage's garden and was standing on the grassy bank of the Sparkling Silver Stream, staring in disbelief. The Sparkling Silver Stream was gone.

All that remained was a damp, brown path, where the Sparkling Silver Stream once had been. Tassel's little brown boat was still tied to the reeds where he had left it, but was now high and dry. There was no water. Tassel decided to find it and he began to walk in the damp path that was all that was left of the Sparkling Silver Stream. He had been to the place where the Sparkling Silver Stream came up from the earth between two big stones once before, and he knew it would be a very long walk. He could fly to the beginning of the Sparkling Silver Stream in half the time, but he didn't want to miss any clues as to what had happened to it.

He had been walking most of the morning and not seen anything unusual except that the Sparkling Silver Stream was not there, where it should be. He was coming into sight of Sparkle's underwater cave except it wasn't underwater any more. Sparkle was standing on the bank of the dried up Sparkling Silver Stream. She was dressed in a pale lemon gown, with a light blue ribbon at her waist. Her golden hair flowed around her shoulders and her blue eyes matched the ribbon at her waist. Her almost transparent wings looked beautiful in the sunshine. When Tassel was close enough, she called to him.

'Where has it gone?' she asked.

Tassel answered, 'I don't know yet, but I'm going to the place where it comes up through the ground between the two big stones. I must find out what has happened to it. The Sparkling Silver Stream brings life itself to the Green Woodland.'

Just then, Michael the leprechaun stepped out of the Green Woodland's undergrowth. He was dressed in emerald green from head to foot, except for his brown leather belt with it's gold buckle and his boots, which were also brown.

He greeted Sparkle and Tassel, 'I have a big problem,' he said. Then he asked, 'Where is the Sparkling Silver Stream?'

'I'm trying to find it,' answered Tassel.

Sparkle asked Michael, 'Apart from losing the Sparkling Silver Stream, what other problem is there?'

Michael spoke, 'My problem isn't as bad as losing the Sparkling Silver Stream, but if I don't put things right soon, I may be sent back to the Master Shoemaker's Workshop, to make and repair shoes and boots.'

'What has happened that you would be taken from the Green

Woodland?' asked Tassel.

'Someone has found my crock of gold and used one of the three wishes. If they use the other two before I can get the crock back, I will find myself learning to be a leprechaun again in the Master Shoemaker's workshop, and that can be a very long time,' said Michael, the smile long gone from his face.

'I have to find the Sparkling Silver Stream,' said Tassel.

'We will all look for the Sparkling Silver Stream,' said Sparkle.

'We will find your crock of gold too,' added Tassel.

So the three little people set off in search of the Sparkling Silver Stream.

Chapter Two

They walked for most of the afternoon. At last, they came to the place where the Sparkling Silver Stream should have been coming up through the earth between the two big stones. There was a tiny drop of water seeping between the two big stones, but it was soon lost into what was left of the brown, damp bed of the Sparkling Silver Stream.

'I have to find out what is stopping the Sparkling Silver Stream from flowing between the two big stones,' said Tassel.

'How can you get through that tiny space between the two big stones?' asked Michael.

Tassel touched the Magical Golden Belt that was around his waist and he dissolved into a small bright, white cloud. Michael and Sparkle watched as the last little bit of the white cloud vanished between the two big stones.

'I have never seen him do that before,' said Michael.

'He has turned himself into a will-o-the-wisp,' stated Sparkle.

'Haven't you noticed he can do so much more since he went to see the Great Wizard?' she added.

Michael and Sparkle sat on the soft green grass next to the two big stones and waited for their friend to return.

Tassel, still in his new form as a will-o-the-wisp, soon found that the Sparkling Silver Stream was no longer flowing out between the two big stones, because it was being drawn through the very small underground passage.

Tassel glided along the surface of the Sparkling Silver Stream like a white mist, until at last he found himself at the top of a small waterfall, emerging into the main cavern of the goblin caves. The water was falling into a large pond that the goblins had dug out to catch it.

Tassel floated over the waterfall and then began to drift around the cavern. One of the goblins shouted, 'It's a will-o-the-wisp!' Another goblin yelled, 'Get it away from me!' and then Tassel found the secret to the stolen stream.

Sitting on his throne was the Hobgoblin King, and beside him was Michael's crock of gold. Tassel floated in front of the Hobgoblin King.

'I am not afraid of you,' he stated.

The shimmering white cloud transformed itself into Tassel the elf, dressed in blue with red boots and red hat. Around his waist was the Magical Golden Belt. 'You should be,' said Tassel.

'I have the leprechaun's crock of gold, I can do anything,' boasted the Hobgoblin King.

'Then it was you who stole the Sparkling Silver Stream,' said Tassel.

'Making the stream come here was easy, but look how the water overflows from the pond, through the underground passage and out into the Great Meadow.' The Hobgoblin King smiled, 'It will turn the Great Meadow into a Great Marsh, and the Great Wizard himself will sink beneath it.'

The Hobgoblin King's voice was loud and echoed around the cavern. 'And this I wish now,' he said. He touched the crock of gold and it glowed. The second wish was granted.

Back at the two big stones, Michael and Sparkle were still waiting for Tassel. Suddenly Michael said, 'Oh no! That's the second wish gone! One more and I will be gone!'

As soon as Tassel realised the second wish was granted, he knew he had very little time to save the Great Wizard. He touched his Magical Golden Belt and was immediately transformed into a flash of lightning. The lightning flashed through the goblin caves and out into the Great Meadow, which was rapidly changing into the Great Marsh.

The wood nymphs who lived in the Great Meadow, were in no immediate danger, for they were so light they could skip across the water if they needed to. But the Great Wizard was different. Although the Great Wizard had great magical power, he had been taken by surprise, and the wish from the crock of gold was very strong. Tassel, in the form of a lightning flash, raced out over the Great Marsh. He saw the Great Wizard being sucked into the muddy water. He guided the flash of lightning to pass over the Great Wizard and, as it did so, Tassel's arms reach out of it and grabbed the Great Wizard from the muddy marsh.

The flash of lightning slowed down, and the Great Wizard and Tassel, (for now Tassel had resumed his normal figure), landed safely on the other side of the Great Marsh, close to the Green Woodland.

'It's the Hobgoblin King at work again,' said Tassel, 'sorry I have to leave you so soon, I must go back to my two friends.'

'That would be Michael and Sparkle,' said the Great Wizard.

'Yes,' answered Tassel. He touched his Magical Golden Belt and flew up into the sky. The Great Wizard waved and then Tassel was gone.

When he arrived back at the two big stones, he was just in time to see Sparkle vanish and Michael being tossed into the sky at a great speed. Tassel didn't know where Sparkle had gone but he could still see Michael, so he tried to follow him, but he couldn't fly fast enough. Then Tassel saw Michael start to fall into a Spiral of Spinning Sparkling Stars. Tassel heard Michael call him as he tumbled helplessly through the neverending tube of spinning stars.

Then Tassel had an idea. He touched his Magical Golden Belt and turned himself into a whirlwind. He soon picked up a lot of speed twisting around and around, just like the Spiral of Spinning Sparkling Stars.

He was getting closer and closer to Michael. For the next part of his plan, he had to be very, very, close to Michael. When the time was just right, Tassel touched his Magical Golden Belt and changed his form again, this time into a beautiful golden eagle. He grabbed Michael's belt with his talons and, with five or six flaps of his tremendously strong wings, he broke free from the Spiral of Spinning Sparkling Stars.

Spreading his massively strong wings, in no time at all they glided back to the entrance of the goblin caves. Just before landing, Tassel changed his form again, from the golden eagle that he had enjoyed being so much, back to his normal figure of Tassel the elf.

'How do you do that?' asked Michael, 'and how do you do the will-o-the-wisp?'

'It's a long story,' said Tassel.

'Why are we outside the goblin caves?' asked Michael.

'The Hobgoblin King has your crock of gold,' answered Tassel.

Chapter Three

The two little people entered the dark caves and kept on walking until they came to the main cavern. The Sparkling Silver Stream was still pouring in and making a beautiful waterfall. The pond that the goblins had made was still overflowing and the water was still being lost through the underground passage and draining into what was now the Great Marsh. The Hobgoblin King was seated on his throne. The crock of gold near his feet had stopped glowing. Michael and Tassel walked over to him and stood in front of him.

'You used the last wish,' Tassel said.

'Yes I did. You can have the old crock now if you want it.'

Michael picked it up.

'What are you doing here?' the Hobgoblin King asked, pointing at Michael. 'You should have been sent somewhere for a hundred years, shouldn't you?'

'Yes,' answered Michael, 'but, I don't think the crock of gold was found fairly. How did you find it?'

'I don't mind telling you,' said the Hobgoblin King, 'I recognised you for what you are, a leprechaun and, eventually, I watched you hide the crock of gold.'

'That is cheating,' said Michael.

The Hobgoblin King smiled. 'All the wishes are used up,' he said, 'and my last wish made everything just right for us. The first wish brought us the stream, the second removed the Great Wizard and the third wish put magic into my waterfall.'

When Tassel looked a little closer, he could see Sparkle trapped inside a glass lantern behind the waterfall.

'Her magic will grant wishes to anyone who drinks water from the pool,' explained the Hobgoblin King.

'As you have given the old crock back to me,' said Michael, 'I had better hide it again.' He made his way across the cavern, pushing his way between the assembled goblins. He stepped onto the rim of the overflowing pond and started to climb the rock face behind the waterfall. As he passed Sparkle he said, 'I will come back for you.'

He climbed to the top of the waterfall and entered the dark passage. He waded through the water until the passage was so small even he was too big to go on any more. He placed his old crock in the tiny hole that the water was flowing through. Then lying on his back, he pushed with his feet, forcing the old crock into the hole as tight as he could, and then he stamped it in, good and tight. The water that was passing the old crock was now only a trickle. Then Michael's crock of gold began to glow again.

The water had to find another way out, so it went back to doing what it had done since it first pushed its way out of the earth, between the two big stones. It began finding its way back through the Green Woodland once again, bringing life and beauty to everything it touched. It wasn't long before the Sparkling Silver Stream was once again flowing from the far side of the Green Woodland, down to the sea.

Michael started to make his way back through the dark passage. When he looked back the crock of gold was glowing brightly. Though Michael didn't know it, the first wish had been undone because Tassel had saved the Great Wizard from the Great Marsh, and now Michael had restored the Sparkling Silver Stream to its rightful place. No wonder the crock of gold was glowing! Now there was only one more wish to undo.

Michael made his way back to where the waterfall had been. It was now only a trickle and not a waterfall any more. Michael climbed down a little way, and then reached across to the lantern and opened the little door.

Sparkle spread her wings and flew out saying, 'Thank you, Michael,' as she passed him.

Suddenly Michael felt much stronger. With Sparkle's freedom, the last wish was undone. Michael couldn't see it, but his crock of gold was glowing brightly.

Michael climbed down the last part of the rock face, and walked around the pond that by now had stopped overflowing. He stood next to Tassel and Sparkle in front of the Hobgoblin King. Michael spoke first, 'All your wishes have been undone. My magic crock of gold is where no one can find it. I will tell you where it is, but you must not move it,' he warned them. 'It's way up there.' He pointed to what was left of the waterfall. 'It is stopping the Sparkling Silver Stream from flooding your caves.'

The Hobgoblin King interrupted him, 'There isn't enough water to flood my caves,' he said.

'There wasn't, but there is now,' said Michael. 'The water that is passing the crock of gold is magical. I have asked the crock to send as much water as it needs to flood the caves, if anyone moves it, and it will,' said Michael.

Then Tassel spoke, 'I can offer you an alternative,' he said.

The Hobgoblin King didn't like what was being said, but he listened and said, 'Tell me your alternative.'

Tassel explained. 'You can keep the pond. The water that falls into it will have magical properties. But there won't be a waterfall. Anyone who drinks from the pond may have a wish. But the magic from the pond will only work inside your caves. Whatever you wish for will disappear as soon as you leave the caves'.

'All right!' said the Hobgoblin King. He could see his plan was not going to work. Well, not all of it.

'We will leave you now, Your Majesty,' said Michael. The three little people turned and passed between the assembled goblins.

'You will never cross the Great Marsh,' the Hobgoblin King called after them.

Sparkle whispered to Michael, 'It's outside the caves, it should be the Great Meadow again by now.'

Chapter Four

They stepped out of the goblin caves and walked to the edge of the Great Meadow. The sun had already risen in the blue sky.

'About mid morning, I think,' said Tassel.

Michael and Sparkle agreed. The three friends started to cross through the long grass that still had yellow and white buttercups and daisies scattered across it. They could hear the wood nymphs chattering to each other, occasionally understanding what they said. Such things as 'She's the fairy of the Sparkling Silver Stream,' and, 'He lives much further downstream, in a little cottage. I think.'

The three friends smiled as they listened. They were just about to leave the Great Meadow and enter the Green Woodland, when a wood nymph stepped out in front of them. It was light green in colour with brown hair, and golden eyes.

'Tassel,' it said, 'I would like to thank you for saving the Great Wizard.'

'I am sure anyone in my place would have done the same,' said Tassel.

'But it wasn't just anyone, it was you,' persisted the wood nymph, then it vanished.

Michael said, 'I think the Great Wizard should have thanked you himself.'

'You know Michael, I heard once, some time ago, that a Great Wizard can be anything. Even a wood nymph,' answered Tassel.

'Oh,' muttered Michael as he suddenly realised he had been in the presence of the Great Wizard.

'I have always had a feeling that we are not so much being

watched, but being looked after,' said Sparkle.

They walked on past the little Woodland Cottage and it wasn't long before they arrived at the Sparkling Silver Stream.

'Doesn't it look beautiful?' said Sparkle.

Michael and Tassel agreed. Then Tassel said, 'Michael, your crock of gold is safe where no one can get to it.'

'That is right,' answered Michael.

'So you are safe here in the Green Woodland and, Sparkle, you have the Sparkling Silver Stream back, so you are once again the fairy of the Silver Stream. The Hobgoblin King is in his caves, and his magic shouldn't spill out beyond the caves. So everything is as it should be.'

'Yes, everything in the Green Woodland is so beautiful again,' said Sparkle.

'If you don't mind, I shall go home and rest. I am feeling very tired,' said Tassel.

'I think I shall do the same,' said Sparkle.

'And me,' added Michael.

They said goodbye until another day, then Tassel touched his Magical Golden Belt, and flew up into the sky. He touched it again and vanished.

Tassel looked down on this wonderful place. The Great Meadow never looked more beautiful, the Green Woodland more peaceful. The only movement below was the Sparkling Silver Stream, with Michael and Sparkle walking side by side along its grassy bank.

'Everything is as it should be,' thought Tassel, as he glided above this beautiful place in the direction of home.

Michael and Sparkle looked into the beautiful clear blue sky, but they couldn't see Tassel. Michael turned to Sparkle and said, 'Do you think he is a...'

Sparkle interrupted him saying, 'No, not yet. He is still our friend, Tassel the elf.

7. The Treasure Chest of Magic

Chapter One

The Hobgoblin King was slumbering in his warm, comfortable bed in his chamber, deep inside the goblin caves. In his dreams he was standing in the Great Meadow, in the centre of a very large, dark green fairy ring. He was making a wish.

'I wish,' he murmured in his sleep, 'for a leprechaun named Brian' he went on. 'Brian, you must do my bidding,' he said, quite clearly. 'Follow the Silver Stream down to the sea.'

The Hobgoblin King snored a deep breath in, then his lips vibrated together, making a 'Zzz...aah' kind of sound as he breathed out.

'Go into the Sea Queen's caves and bring to me the Treasure Chest of Magic. You will only be free from my wish when this task is done.'

A few moments passed as the Hobgoblin King slept. Then the silence was broken when a very excited goblin burst into the King's chamber.

'Your Majesty! Your Majesty!' he shouted, waking the Hobgoblin King from his slumber.

'What is it?' the Hobgoblin King asked as he opened his eyes, his dream still running through his mind.

'Your Majesty, I went out early this morning looking for mushrooms in the Great Meadow, and instead of mushrooms, I found a very big fairy circle.'

The Hobgoblin King rubbed his eyes. 'Lead me to it,' he said as he dressed himself in a dark green shirt and trousers. He pulled his black boots on and pulled tight the black leather belt at his waist.

The Hobgoblin King and a few other goblins from the goblin band followed the first goblin that had first brought news of the fairy ring. They walked a little way into the Great Meadow and then the first goblin said, 'Here it is.' He was pointing at the dark ring of grass.

'This looks familiar,' thought the Hobgoblin King. He stepped into the circle and moved to the centre.

'I wish for a leprechaun named Brian,' he said. All was quite for a moment then, before the Hobgoblin King's eyes, suddenly appeared a leprechaun. He was dressed from head to foot in dark green, with the exception of a brown belt with a silver buckle and brown boots. He had a beaming face and bushy eyebrows.

'Brian,' said the Hobgoblin King, 'you must do my bidding.'

This surprised the Hobgoblin King, for he was saying exactly what he had said in his dream.

'Follow the Silver Stream down to the sea. Go to the Sea Queen's caves and bring to me the Treasure Chest of Magic. You will only be free from my wish when this task is completed.'

Brian bowed to the Hobgoblin King, 'I shall return,' he said.

'The Silver Stream is that way,' said the Hobgoblin King. He was pointing in the direction of the Green Woodland. He watched until Brian the leprechaun had left the Great Meadow and entered the Green Woodland.

'Your Majesty,' said one of the goblins, 'what is the Treasure Chest of Magic?'

The Hobgoblin King answered, 'I don't really know, I dreamed about it and if it is magical, I want it.'

'Of course, Your Majesty,' the goblin replied.

The Hobgoblin King and his band of goblins started to make their way back to the goblin caves, not knowing that they had started a chain of events that even the Great Wizard would not be able to stop.

Chapter Two

Brian walked for some time, passing the little Woodland Cottage and entering the Green Woodland. It wasn't long before he found the Sparkling Silver Stream and started to follow it to the sea. He had been walking along the grassy bank for some time when suddenly he saw something flying very close to the water. Although his knowledge of life was quite considerable it wasn't complete, as he had been taken away from his Master before his education had been completed. This was why his clothes were dark green instead of emerald green. Brian sat down on the grassy bank of the Silver Stream and watched the shining object that had caught his eye.

'Is it a damselfly?' he thought. 'No, it's a dragonfly,' he said to himself.

Then the object flew towards him and he changed his mind again.

'It is a butterfly,' he said out loud. The object stopped in front of him and hovered in the air, just above the surface of the water.

'Hello,' it said, 'you are new here.'

Brian stared at the shining figure. 'You are a fairy,' he said, never taking his eyes from her.

'Yes, my name is Sparkle, and I am the fairy of the Sparkling Silver Stream.'

Sparkle had long, flowing, golden hair and she wore a gown of silvery blue that matched the surface of the Sparkling Silver Stream.

'You look like part of the Silver Stream,' said Brian, still not taking his eyes from the shining figure. Sparkle landed on the soft, green grass next to Brian, her transparent wings glistening in the sunlight.

'Who are you?' she asked.

'I am Brian. I am a leprechaun,' he said. 'Well, almost a leprechaun,' he added.

'Where did you come from?' she asked.

'I came from Nowhere,' answered Brian. 'I don't know what really happened. I was suddenly whisked away from all I knew and found myself in a fairy ring with some goblins, in a place called the Great Meadow.'

'You came from Nowhere?' said a voice from behind them.

It was Michael. He had been sitting on the grass behind them and had heard every word of their conversation. He was dressed in emerald green with a brown leather belt with a gold buckle and matching brown leather boots.

'Yes,' said Brian, as he turned to see where the voice had come from. 'You are a leprechaun,' he said, looking at the figure in green.

'That I am,' answered Michael.

Sparkle interrupted them with a question, 'Where is Nowhere?' she asked.

'I don't know,' answered Brian.

'Nowhere is a place we come from, and don't want to go back to,' explained Michael, 'I nearly went back once, but I was saved by a golden eagle.'

Brian listened intently and then asked, 'Who are you?'

'I am Michael, the leprechaun. This is Sparkle, the fairy of the Sparkling Silver Stream and we live here, in the Green Woodland.'

Michael looked closely at Brian. 'You are not a leprechaun yet. Where did you get those eyebrows? And why are you here?' he asked.

'I was summoned from Nowhere, by a dark green goblin and told to retrieve the Treasure Chest of Magic. I must get it from wherever it is, and take it to wherever he is,' explained Brian.

'Well, I know where it is, but we could never retrieve it,' said Michael.

'We shouldn't even try,' said Sparkle, 'we know how dangerous it is.'

'We also know the Hobgoblin King, the one who sent you after it,' added Michael.

'But...' exclaimed Brian, 'I can't do anything until I place the Treasure Chest of Magic into the hands of the Hobgoblin King.'

'We must find Tassel,' said Sparkle.

Tassel was the elf that lived in the little cottage along the bank of the Sparkling Silver Stream, closer to the sea. This seemed a good idea to Michael and Brian, so the three little people began their journey to the little cottage to find Tassel.

Chapter Three

The journey had taken most of the morning and a little of the afternoon. Michael and Sparkle had explained to Brian all about Tassel as they had walked along the bank of the Sparkling Silver Stream. They also told him the story in detail of the Treasure Chest of Magic.

'If we were to retrieve it, I can't give it to the Hobgoblin King,' Brian said abruptly. He had been thinking deeply about what Michael and Sparkle had been telling him.

'If we don't,' Michael explained, pointing at Brian, 'then you will not become a leprechaun and you will wander aimlessly until this wish that the Hobgoblin King set for you is granted.'

'So I won't be a leprechaun, and will not do anything with my magical lifetime,' said Brian.

As the three little people approached the little cottage, they saw Tassel tying his little brown boat to some reeds. Tassel was dressed in a blue shirt and trousers with red boots and red hat. Around his waist was a Magical Golden Belt. Brian felt quite excited when he saw Tassel, for he had heard such a lot about him from Michael and Sparkle. He could hardly wait to know if Tassel would help him.

Tassel observed the three little people walking towards him. He knew one was Sparkle, for she could not be mistaken for anything else than the fairy of the Sparkling Silver Stream. The figure in emerald green was Michael, but the third figure, not as tall as Michael and dressed in dark green, was not someone he had met before. As the figures approached, Michael introduced Brian to Tassel.

'I am pleased to meet you, Brian,' said Tassel.

Michael and Sparkle explained to Tassel how Brian had appeared from Nowhere, and how he had to retrieve the Treasure Chest of Magic, and give it to the Hobgoblin King before he could go back to wherever he had come from.

Tassel suggested that they should use his little brown boat to reach the Sandy Beach and the sea. It took most of the afternoon to reach the Sandy Beach. During that time, Brian explained how one day he would like to be a leprechaun like Michael, and how he has been waiting for his clothes to change to emerald green. The journey passed quite quickly while Tassel, Michael and Sparkle listened to Brian.

When they reached the end of the Sparkling Silver Stream and the sea, Tassel and Michael jumped out of the little brown boat and pushed it out of the water, and onto the sandy beach. Brian climbed out of the boat and Sparkle flew over his head.

'This way,' said Tassel.

The four fairy folk set out across the beach, towards the Fairy Sea Queen's caves. They had only taken a few steps when another figure appeared close to Tassel. He was dressed in blue and his eyes were a golden colour. It was Surf, the sea sprite. When Tassel saw him, he started to say, 'Surf! Oh, I mean, Great Wiz...'

Surf interrupted him, 'I am here to help you retrieve the Treasure Chest of Magic.'

'I think the Hobgoblin King is behind this,' said Tassel.

'There is more to this than the Hobgoblin King,' stated Surf.

When they reached the Fairy Sea Queen's caves, Surf said, 'I will wait here for you.'

Tassel, Michael, Sparkle and Brian went inside. It was dark, though Tassel could see very well, as it was just one of the magical powers supplied by his Magical Golden Belt. It wasn't long before Tassel and the other fairy folk reached the Fairy Sea Queen's main cavern. As they entered, the Fairy Sea Queen stepped out of the darkness, and could be seen very clearly with the luminous light given off by the very deep rock pool that supplied all the light in the Fairy Sea Queen's cavern. She had golden hair, and had a dark green cloak around her. Beneath the cloak she wore a dark green blouse and dress with a brown waistcoat with yellow laces. At her wrists were leather guards.

She moved towards them saying, 'Hello, Tassel. I know why you have come. You are the only one able to retrieve the Treasure Chest of Magic. The rock pool is so deep it will be very dangerous, even for you. Your Magical Golden Belt will protect you, but even I don't know what you will find down there.'

'Thank you for letting me try to retrieve it,' said Tassel.

He touched his Magical Golden Belt. There was a yellowish glow all around him, and slowly he started to turn green. Fins started to grow under his arms and at the back of his legs. He felt a strong tingling in the back of his head and he started to choke.

'Quickly,' said the Fairy Sea Queen, 'we must get him into the water.'

Tassel stepped into the rock pool and began to sink. Once he was completely under the water the tingling stopped in his head. He could breathe the water in through is nose, like air, and blow it out through his mouth. Michael, Sparkle and Brian watched until they couldn't see him anymore. As soon as Tassel understood how his new powers worked he started to dive, down, down, down, deeper and deeper.

The fins under his arms and at the back of his legs gave him great speed as he continued to go deeper and deeper. His Magical Golden Belt gave him the ability to see in the darkness. It was invaluable to him. He had not swam in any direction, only straight down. Now, still far below him, he could see the Treasure Chest of Magic. He swam deeper, getting closer to his prize. As he approached the Treasure Chest, he realised, but too late, that the Treasure Chest was on a little ledge.

The movement of the water, as he moved through it, disturbed the Treasure Chest, and it slipped off the ledge and began to sink even deeper. Tassel called on all the speed his fins could give him, but just then he caught sight of something far below him. His sight was very good, which meant he could see quite well even under the water. What he saw gave him a terrible fright.

It was big, and it was black and gold, and it was coming up.

Tassel couldn't let the Treasure Chest of Magic be lost, and so he swam on down towards this monster of the deep. The black·and gold (whatever it may be) seemed to be getting bigger. The Treasure Chest of Magic seemed to be sinking faster than Tassel could swim, and it looked like he would have to return to the surface of the rock pool.

The black and gold monster of the deep circled round and round below him. Suddenly this very large fish-like creature blew a very large bubble out of its mouth. It floated up towards Tassel engulfing the Treasure Chest of Magic as it rose. Then the bubble engulfed Tassel. It carried Tassel and the Treasure Chest almost to the surface, then it burst, leaving Tassel holding the Treasure Chest.

He breathed in lots of water, and blew it out through his mouth. It didn't refresh him as air would, but it would have to do.

Now that Tassel had the Treasure Chest of Magic, he looked up. He could see the surface of the rock pool. He started swimming up towards the light. As he ascended through the water the light became brighter. He held the Treasure Chest of Magic close to him with one arm, using his other arm and legs to push his way to the surface of the water. It seemed a long time, but at last he found himself in the air of the cavern, with his friends, Michael, Sparkle, Brian and the Fairy Sea Queen. Tassel touched his Magical Golden Belt and his fins vanished. Then he sucked in a very big breath of air.

'Oh! That is so much better than water,' he said. His green colouring faded and was replaced with blue.

The Fairy Sea Queen let Tassel recover from his very wet adventure and then she said, 'Tassel, you and your friends must take the Treasure Chest of Magic to the goblin caves. When you get there, give the Treasure Chest to Brian. Let him give it to the Hobgoblin King. You must do this if Brian is to return to wherever he came from.'

'Where did he come from?' asked Tassel.

'He came from Nowhere,' answered the Fairy Sea Queen.

'Where is Nowhere?' asked Tassel.

'I can't tell you, but you will find it,' answered the Fairy Sea Queen.

'How do you know about Brian and his task?' asked Tassel.

Sparkle spoke before the Fairy Sea Queen could answer, 'Surf, the sea sprite told you, didn't he, Your Majesty?'

The Fairy Sea Queen looked at Tassel, 'Yes, he did,' she answered.

'You know about Surf?' said Tassel.

'Yes, I do,' answered the Fairy Sea Queen, 'He told me to keep the key to the Treasure Chest of Magic. If the Hobgoblin King manages to keep the Treasure Chest he will not be able to open it.'

'Thank you for keeping the Treasure Chest safe. It is up to us now, and we will all do our best to see that the Treasure Chest of Magic is placed in the right hands,' said Tassel.

'That may not be easily done,' said the Fairy Sea Queen. 'You had better start your journey to the goblin caves. But remember, Tassel, you are always welcome here.'

They all thanked the Fairy Sea Queen and then found their way through the caves to the sandy beach. When they stepped out into the mid afternoon sunshine, Surf the sea sprite was waiting for them.

As soon as Michael saw him, he said, 'You are a Wiz...' He was interrupted by Tassel. 'Sea sprite,' he said.

'Yes, I am a sea sprite,' said Surf.

'You wouldn't know anything about a black and gold monster of the deep that really frightened me, would you?' asked Tassel.

'I know the monster gave you the Treasure Chest of Magic, and pushed you as far as I could to the surface of the rock pool,' said Surf.

'What monster?' asked Michael.

'I will tell you and Sparkle when we find time to rest,' said Tassel. Surf walked with the four fairy folk and helped them get Tassel's little brown boat off the sand and into the water.

Before they started their journey, Surf said, 'When you get to the goblin caves, Brian, I want you to give the Treasure Chest of Magic to the Hobgoblin King. This will release you from his wish. Then Tassel, I want you to take it back from the Hobgoblin King. Then you and Michael are to take it to...' There was a silence. The four little people waited to hear what was next. Then to Michael's dismay, Surf said, 'the Master Shoemaker.'

Michael frowned, his smile long since gone. 'If we go in there, we won't get out again,' he said.

'I will try to help you,' said Surf.

'The Great Wizard himself could not get us out of the Master Shoemaker's workshop,' said Michael.

Tassel helped his friends into his boat, then whispered to Surf, 'We will do it somehow.'

Surf touched Tassel's arm. 'I will help you,' he said. His eyes glowing a golden warmth of friendship.

'I know you will. Thank you, Great Wizard,' said Tassel.

Chapter Four

The journey to Sparkle's Magical Cave passed quite quickly. During this time Tassel, Michael and Sparkle explained to Brian all about the Treasure Chest of Magic. Now Brian understood why the Hobgoblin King wanted it. The magic within it was very powerful and must not be set free.

Tassel was first to jump from his little brown boat to the grassy bank of the Sparkling Silver Stream. He tied his little brown boat to some reeds and then the other little people climbed onto the grassy bank. Michael showed Brian the way into Sparkle's cave through the small hole between the roots of the willow tree. When Michael and Brian arrived in the Magical Cave the others were already there. They had used magic to enter the cave. Brian looked around. The cave was spherical, the walls were grey rock with pieces of silver and gold in it, but one side was open to the Sparkling, Silver Stream. Brian looked in wonder at the side of the cave that was water. His big bushy eyebrows were as high as he could make them go.

'What is stopping the water coming in?' he asked.

Michael and Tassel said nothing. 'It is magic,' said Sparkle.

'This is one of the most enchanted places in the Green

Woodland,' added Michael as he placed the Treasure Chest of Magic on the little table.

Brian was looking at himself in the very big mirror that was opposite the wall of water, 'It makes the cave look much bigger, doesn't it?' he said.

'Oh it does.' said Michael 'We used it once to put a Rainbow into the sky over the Black Forest.'

'Where is the Black Forest?' asked Brian, his eyebrows moving up and down with excitement.

'Some time ago,' said Michael 'the Green Woodland was turned into the Black Forest by a Black Crystal...'

Sparkle interrupted him. 'I hope you will excuse me. I am going to sleep and I think you should do the same. The morning will come very soon and we all have things to do.' She opened a little door near the mirror. 'Sleep well,' she said as she closed it behind her.

'I never knew that door was there,' said Michael with surprise.

'A bedroom, I think,' said Tassel.

Brian and Michael talked for a long time into the night. By the time they fell asleep Brian had heard most of the adventures that Michael, Sparkle and Tassel had shared.

When morning came Sparkle found her friends still asleep on the floor of her cave. She woke them gently one by one saying it was time to go to the goblin caves. Once they were all awake, Sparkle gave her friends some breakfast of mushrooms and warm butter milk. It wasn't long before they started their walk through the Green Woodland.

As they passed the Woodland Cottage Brian remarked, 'It is difficult to believe that this was the Black Castle.'

'Yes, it is.' answered Michael.

Brian's eyebrows rose higher than when he had been told about the Black Witch. They moved past the little Woodland Cottage and into the Great Meadow. Most of the morning had been spent walking and talking, with Michael carrying the Treasure Chest of Magic. But now, as they crossed the Great Meadow, they spoke in whispers. Soon they were outside the goblin caves.

Michael gave Brian the Treasure Chest of Magic. Brian held it tightly with both hands and they went in. As they approached the main cavern they could hear the goblins laughing and talking. Tassel touched Brian's arm and whispered, 'When he asks you for it, you give it to him.' Brian nodded.

Then Tassel whispered to Sparkle, 'If I can't get it away from the Hobgoblin King, you make him drop it with magic.'

Sparkle nodded to let Tassel know she understood.

'What shall I do?' asked Michael.

'You will deliver the Treasure Chest of Magic safely into the hands of the Master Shoemaker,' answered Tassel.

Chapter Five

They entered the main cavern and the laughing and talking stopped. As soon as the Hobgoblin King noticed them he stood up and said, 'Make way for them. They are bringing me my dream come true - the Treasure Chest of Magic.'

The four little people stood in front of the Hobgoblin King. He held out his hands 'MINE!' he exclaimed.

'Go on Brian, give him the Treasure Chest,' urged Tassel.

Brian did what he was asked and as soon as the Hobgoblin King held the Treasure Chest of Magic in his hands, Brian vanished. This startled the Hobgoblin King.

'Where has he gone?' he asked.

'Back where he came from,' answered Tassel.

'And where is that?' he asked, louder than before.

'Nowhere,' said Michael and Tassel together.

The Hobgoblin King tried to open the Treasure Chest, 'Where is the key?' he asked.

'I can truly say I haven't seen it since it was locked,' said Tassel.

'I will break it open!' snarled the Hobgoblin King.

'I wouldn't try that,' said Tassel as he snatched the Treasure Chest from the Hobgoblin King.

'Give that back!' he shouted.

Just then one of the other goblins grabbed Sparkle and roughly threw her into a four-sided, black, glass lantern. In doing so he ripped one of her wings then he slammed the door shut.

'Give back the Treasure Chest or your stream fairy will spend the rest of her life granting the wish of light for us in our caves,' he said.

'We can't give him the Treasure Chest, we don't know what damage he could do with it,' Michael said anxiously.

Tassel called to Sparkle, 'I will get you out Sparkle.' He touched his Magical Golden Belt and, with one arm holding the Treasure Chest and the other around Michael, he flew just over the heads of the assembled goblins at such a speed that they could only just see him. Through the passages of the goblin caves he flew, and out only slowing down enough to see the Great Meadow below them.

Tassel gave the Treasure Chest of Magic to Michael. 'Now we must take it to the Master Shoemaker,' he said.

'You mean we are going to Nowhere?' said Michael. 'You know we will lose all our magical powers?'

'I know,' said Tassel. 'The Great Wizard said he would try to help me.'

So with Tassel and Michael increasing in speed, it wasn't long before the sky darkened and a Spiral of Spinning Sparkling Stars, came into sight.

'If we go in, there is no way out,' said Michael.

'Hold onto the Treasure Chest,' said Tassel.

They entered the Spiral of Spinning Sparkling Stars.

Chapter Six

It was like sliding down a very big slide. The faster they travelled, the dizzier they felt. It was so pretty, just like being inside a kaleidoscope. Dancing colours, gold and silver stars. Then quite suddenly they entered what looked like a white cloud. They slowed down, almost coming to a stop, and then fell out of the cloud landing in the middle of the Master Shoemaker's workshop. Their heads cleared quite quickly and what they saw was wonderful. The workshop was filled with work benches. There were lots of little men, all working on all kinds of footwear. Boots, shoes, clogs and slippers. They were all dressed the same, that is in dark green. Michael recognised one of the little men. He was working on a pair of ballet shoes. When he saw Michael he stopped what he was doing and walked over to greet him. When Tassel saw him, he recognised him too.

'Brian!' said Tassel. 'I would recognise those eyebrows anywhere.'

Brian started to ask how they came to be in the Master Shoemaker's workshop when silence spread across this magical place. Michael and Tassel turned to see the Master Shoemaker himself.

'I am sorry, I don't know how to address you,' said Tassel.

'Sir,' said Michael. 'You call him Sir.'

'He is right,' said the Master Shoemaker. 'I think you have something for me, Tassel.'

'You know me?' Tassel took a gulp of air, 'sir?'

'Yes, I know about your adventures. You remind me of...' the Shoemaker paused, '...me,' he said. 'Yes, you remind me of me.'
A smile flooded across his face.

Tassel had never seen anything like the Master Shoemaker before, or perhaps once before, when he had seen the Great Wizard in the Great Meadow. It certainly felt the same.

The Master Shoemaker had a round face with blue eyes. He wore a monocle. This was so that he could see the very tiny stitches that he put into his work. The other eye watched over his workshop and the magical little people in it. He had a silver grey beard and wore a leather apron. He was dressed in green, not emerald green, but a sparkling, shining kind of green. On his feet he wore a pair of very shiny black shoes, each with a shining Golden Buckle.

Michael and Tassel looked around them.

'Isn't Nowhere a wonderful place?' Brian asked softly.

'Yes it is,' answered Tassel, who looked at Michael. 'This is a wonderful place. Why did you not want to come here?'

'Because we lost all our magic getting here and, without it, we cannot leave,' Michael answered. 'We can't leave, can we?' Michael asked the Master Shoemaker as he gave him the Treasure Chest of Magic.

'I am not allowed to help anyone leave, not even you, and I know you both have done a great service to all fairy folk in bringing the Treasure Chest of Magic to me. It will never leave here, and it will never be opened.'

'Isn't there anyway that you can send them back?' asked Brian.

'All the magic they possessed was used to get them here, that is why no one leaves without me knowing about it,' said the Master Shoemaker.

'But Tassel,' the Master Shoemaker added, 'getting here drained all your magic.' He moved close to Tassel and whispered in his ear, 'But not the magic in your belt.'

'Do you think it has enough power to take Michael and me through the Spiral of Spinning Sparkling Stars?' asked Tassel.

'You can only try,' said the Master Shoemaker.

'Thank you, sir,' said Tassel.

The Master Shoemaker spoke once more. 'Tassel, there are three great forces to help you; the Great Wizard, the Fairy Sea Queen and...' There was a pause. 'Me,' he added. 'If I can help you to look after the Green Woodland, I will. One day I will send your friend Brian to you. When he is ready he will be a good leprechaun. Now go. You too, Michael. If I see you again you will be here for one hundred years.'

'Can I go with them?' asked Brian.

'No,' came the answer, as the Master Shoemaker shook his head. 'You are not ready yet, but you will meet the fairy folk of the Green Woodland again.'

'I will know you by those eyebrows,' said Michael with a smile.

A white cloud appeared in the middle of the Master Shoemaker's workshop. Tassel and Michael stepped into it and Tassel took a firm grip on Michael and touched his Magical Golden Belt. The two figures vanished from the Master Shoemaker and Brian's sight. The Master Shoemaker thought he heard Tassel say, 'Thank you,' as he vanished.

'The Treasure Chest of Magic will be safe here won't it, sir?' asked Brian.

'It will,' he the replied.

Tassel and Michael emerged from the white cloud into the Spiral of Spinning Sparkling Stars. The spinning stars and flashing colours made them feel quite dizzy. At last, they could see blue sky.

'Just a little more.' said Tassel, but the magic in his belt was all gone. The two little figures started to be pulled back into the Spiral of Spinning Sparkling Stars.

'Oh no!' cried Michael. 'It will be one hundred years this time!'

Then Tassel saw something, it was big, it was black and gold and it was breathing fire from its mouth. Then Michael saw it too.

'Oh no! Not a dragon? I would rather do one hundred years than be eaten by a dragon!'

The dragon flew closer and closer. Then Michael and Tassel were snatched from the Spiral of Spinning Sparkling Stars. They were held tightly in the clawed feet of the dragon and soon found themselves flying with the dragon in the clear, blue sky.

'This isn't so bad,' said Michael.

'No, not so bad,' remarked Tassel.

It wasn't long before they could see the Green Woodland and moments later they landed in the Great Meadow. The dragon transformed into the Great Wizard, his black and gold cloak folded around him. 'Thank you both, Michael and Tassel. That was a brave undertaking that you have just completed,' said the Great Wizard

'Excuse me, Great Wizard, will we get our magical powers back now?' asked Michael.

'I am sorry Michael, not now, but your magical powers will be restored in the passing of time,' answered the Great Wizard.

'Thank you for rescuing us,' said Michael, 'I just have to go home and rest.'

The Great Wizard spoke to Michael again. 'Michael,' he said, 'when you are rested, I would like you to go to the Fairy Sea Queen and ask her for Tassel's silver belt. Then bring it here to the Great Meadow.'

'I will, Great Wizard,' answered Michael.

The two little people had turned to leave, when the Great Wizard said, 'Tassel, I need to explain a few things.'

'Go Michael,' said Tassel 'I will catch you up.'

Michael wandered across the Great Meadow and was lost from their sight. Tassel turned and looked at the Great Wizard.

'What must you tell me?' he asked.

'I am sorry, Tassel. The last adventure is my fault. Please let me explain. Sometime ago I offered you the choice to become a wizard.'

'And I said no thank you, Great Wizard,' said Tassel.

'I should have listened to you, but I didn't. I went ahead and gave you the powers of a wizard. I thought that once you found out what you could do, you would want to become a wizard. But you didn't, and so the Wizards That Be said that in order to have the powers I gave you, you must prove yourself worthy of them. So I gave the Hobgoblin King the dream of the Treasure Chest of Magic. I'm sorry Tassel.' There was a pause as the Great Wizard thought for a moment.

'You have made the Green Woodland much safer, now that the Master Shoemaker has the Treasure Chest of Magic and the Fairy Sea Queen has the key,' he said.

The Great Wizard looked very serious as he explained to Tassel that the Wizards That Be would not allow him to restore his magical powers. 'I gave you too much too soon, but the passing of time will see your magical powers restored.'

Then Tassel asked, 'Can the Fairy Sea Queen help me? She did give me the Golden Magical Belt.'

'I know the Fairy Sea Queen gave you the belt,' said the Great Wizard. 'I think I can do something with it. Tassel, take the belt off and give it to me.'

Tassel did as the Great Wizard asked and gave the belt to him. The Great Wizard looked like he was trying to find something under his black and gold cloak. Then he held out his hand to show Tassel three little crystals. Tassel watched as the Great Wizard pressed them firmly into his belt.

'Here, put this on,' said the Great Wizard, as he gave the belt back to Tassel.

As soon as Tassel put the belt around his waist it began to glow a bright, golden yellow, and the three crystals sparkled.

'As with any gift to do with fairy folk, it is magic. Each crystal carries one wish that will be granted,' said the Great Wizard.

Tassel asked, 'May I use them now?'

'You may, but be careful what you wish for,' warned the Great Wizard.

'My first wish is that Michael is safe in his home, wherever it is, and that he has all of his magical powers restored to him.'

The Magical Golden Belt glowed for a moment, then one of the crystals lost its sparkle and changed its colour to a cloudy blue.

'That is quite a wish,' said the Great Wizard. 'But it is granted,' he said with a smile.

'My second wish...'

But the Great Wizard interrupted him. 'Are you sure you want to use it now?' he asked.

'Oh yes please,' answered Tassel.

'Very well,' he said.

'My second wish is that Sparkle is returned unharmed to her Magical Cave with all her magical powers, and that her damaged wing is as it was before it was torn by the goblins.'

'Is that all?' asked the Great Wizard.

'Yes,' answered Tassel. 'Have I asked for too much, Great Wizard?'

'That is quite a big wish,' came the answer.

Tassel's belt glowed again, and another crystal lost its sparkle and changed its colour to a cloudy blue.

A moment passed, and the Great Wizard said, 'Your wish is granted.'

Tassel thought for a moment and then asked, 'Are you allowed to help me with the last wish?'

'I can only give you advice,' answered the Great Wizard.

'What would your advice be?' asked Tassel.

'You must look for someone who you can offer anything their heart desires, then tell them of your adventures and wait and hope that they will use the last wish to restore your magical powers, so that you may go on looking after the Green Woodland, the Great Meadow, and the Sparkling Silver Stream, as far as the sea.'

'That may take some time,' said Tassel.

'I will watch, and help when I can. You will find a way,' the Great Wizard said reassuringly.

Tassel looked at the Magical Golden Belt and its one sparkling crystal. 'Yes, I will find a way,' he said.

The Great Wizard watched Tassel as he wandered across the Great Meadow, until he lost sight of him as he entered the Green Woodland.

'Yes, you will find a way,' the Great Wizard said to himself.

As the Great Wizard vanished from the Great Meadow he said something else, his words lingering in the air where he had been standing.

'It will be soon. This I promise.'

8. Tassel's Last Adventure

Chapter One

It was a glorious summer morning. I awoke early and looked out of my window. The town was quiet. I packed a small backpack with a drink of soda pop, a sandwich and my cloak, in case the evening became cold. Then I set out on what I hoped would be a very long country walk. It wasn't long before I was out of the town and walking towards the beach. The sky was clear blue, not a cloud in sight and at last I could see the sea. It was the same colour as the sky.

I walked across the warm yellow sand and, although I had been here many times, I had not noticed the little stream flowing out of the Green Woodland.

I stopped walking just to look. It was one of the most beautiful things I had ever seen, sparkling in the morning sunlight. As I looked along the beach beyond the little silver stream, I noticed some caves. I had never noticed them before either, although they must have been there. I decided I would follow the little silver stream into the Green Woodland. So that is what I did.

It wasn't long before I came upon a little cottage nestling in a beautiful garden that seemed to be part of the Green Woodland. I just stood still and looked at it. Though I knew these places very well, they seemed different today. I walked on past the cottage and continued to follow the little silver stream. It wasn't long before I came to a bend in the little stream. There was a very big willow tree on the bank of the stream and the water was trying to flow around it and, in doing so, flowed back onto itself making the little stream very deep at this place.

As I gazed into the deepest part of the stream, I could see what looked like an underwater cave. I knew that was not possible, but there it was. As the water flowed past, the cave would vanish and then reappear again. I spent a lot of time there as the entire place felt different, magical, for I was amazed just looking at it. Quite a long time must have passed when I decided to follow the little stream further into the Green Woodland.

In a while I came to a fork in the little path. One way went around a hill and out of the Green Woodland, so I chose the other path that lead me past a woodland cottage. There was an old lady with grey hair in the garden.

She said, 'Hello,' as I passed. I answered saying, 'Isn't it a beautiful day?' as I went on my way. In a very short time, I found myself leaving the Green Woodland and entering a very big meadow.

The grass wasn't too high and so I walked on. Something, a feeling, was compelling me to walk on. The further I walked into the meadow, the more effort I had to use just to keep walking. I think I must have been about in the centre of the meadow when I stopped walking and looked around me. Everything was quiet, not even a breeze touched my face.

I put my back pack down and sat down next to it. I felt so tired. I leaned against my backpack and gazed up at the sky. It was blue, the sun was shining. I felt at peace. There were too or three fluffy little clouds in the sky. A bee which flew too close to my ear gave me that sound of summer. I breathed in the fresh, summer air, the type of air that carries the perfume of green grass and warm hay.

'Excuse me. Over here! At your feet.'

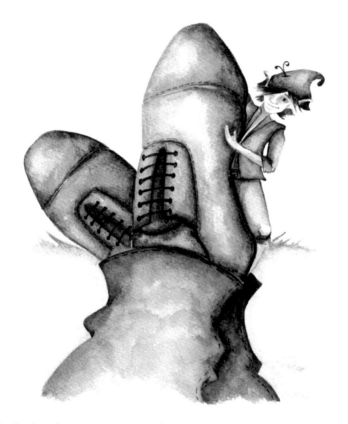

I looked and, to my surprise, there was a little man. He was dressed in blue, with red boots, and a red hat. Around his waist was a golden belt with one sparkling crystal and two cloudy, blue ones.

'You are Mr. Lawrence, aren't you?' he asked.

'Yes, I am,' I said.

'The Great Wizard said I would find you here today,' said the little man.

'When did he tell you that?' I asked.

'Yesterday,' replied the little man.

'I didn't know myself until now, that I would be here today,' I said.

'The Great Wizard knows most things. That is why he sent me. My name is Tassel, I am an elf,' he said.

'Why did he send you?' I asked.

'It is a long story,' said Tassel.

I leaned back against my back pack. 'Please tell me your story, Tassel,' I said.

Chapter Two

Tassel sat on the grass close to me, and then he said, 'It started a long time ago, when a Black Crystal brought a very dark time to us, that is the fairy folk that live in these parts. It darkened everything from the Great Meadow to the sea, it even affected the goblins.'

'You say there are goblins here too?' I asked.

'Oh, yes,' replied Tassel. 'They live just over there in the goblin caves.'

He was pointing at the hill at one side of the Great Meadow. It was the hill I had decided not to walk around.

'The Goblin King and his band were not good to start with and the Black Crystal made them worse. The Black Crystal turned the little Woodland Cottage into the Black Castle and the grey haired old lady into the Black Witch. It turned the Green Woodland into the Black Forest and everything was very bad for all the fairy folk for a long time.'

'Why didn't your Wizard friend stop it?' I asked.

'He couldn't,' came the reply. 'The Sparkling Silver Stream lost it's sparkle. The Great Meadow became a maze. We even lost the wood nymphs from the Great Meadow. But one good thing happened, although it wasn't good for me. One night, the moondust stuck to me and I became the Luminous Elf. I asked the lady who lives in the little cottage where I live if she could help me, and she...'

I interrupted him. 'You have spoken to humans like me before?'

'Only the lady in the cottage. We would only make contact with beings like you if there was no other way,' said Tassel.

'Are you in trouble now?' I asked. There was a pause.

'Yes,' replied Tassel.

'Please tell me the rest of your story,' I said.

Tassel went on, 'The lady said I would find the answer to my problem at the sea. She told me to follow the Silver Stream, and so I did.'

'I never noticed the Silver Stream flowing onto the sandy beach until today,' I said.

'The Great Wizard has allowed you to see many things that your kind should not see,' said Tassel. 'You will see more before the day ends.'

'What happened when you reached the sandy beach?' I asked.

'I was met by a sea sprite who took me to see the Fairy Sea Queen. She freed me from the luminous moondust and poured it into a very deep rock pool that is in her caves. When I returned to the little cottage, I granted three wishes to the lady. They were health, hope and happiness for her two children. All was as well as it could be for some time. Then one day, two elves came to the Black Forest and tried to place a Rainbow over it. But it was hit by lightning and the colours were lost, scattered all over the Black Forest. The real trouble arose when we tried to retrieve the colour purple from the Black Castle. We had followed the Black Witch into the dungeons and, in a fit of rage, she hurled the purple gem at Sparkle...'

I interrupted Tassel again. 'Who is Sparkle?' I asked.

'She is the fairy of the Sparkling Silver Stream,' he answered.

'Even the stream has a fairy?' I said.

157

'Oh, yes,' said Tassel.

'What happened next?' I asked.

'I put myself between Sparkle and the little purple gem. I called on all the magic I ever knew and the little gem split into two and passed either side of us. Then my shadow jumped from the wall, and my reflection rose from the wet floor. It was such a surprise. My shadow caught one of the little gems and my reflection caught the other. They gave the two little gems to me and then vanished. I knew someone or something was looking after me. As yet, I didn't know who or why. We did put the Rainbow into the sky over the Black Forest, using a mirror and the water from the Sparkling Silver Stream. We launched it from Sparkle's underwater cave.'

'Is that where the stream bends around a big willow tree?' I asked.

'Yes, that's the place,' answered Tassel.

'I felt something as I passed it this morning,' I said.

'The Great Wizard will have allowed you to sense it, or even allowed you a glimpse or two. It is a very magical place,' explained Tassel.

I started to move to stand up, when Tassel said, 'There is still more to tell you, Mr. Lawrence.'

I leaned back, resting on my backpack, and the little elf began to speak again.

'Remember I told you about being the Luminous Elf?'

'Yes,' I replied.

'I went back to the lady in the little cottage and granted her three wishes. She didn't want anything for herself but asked if I could grant health, hope and happiness for her two children. This I did. When the children grew up they stopped believing in fairies, and the Goblin King decided to imprison me in a glass snow globe until I withdrew the three wishes. His argument was that I must not grant wishes to beings who don't believe in us. But I couldn't go back on my promise to the lady who had helped me. The glass snow globe was left in a clearing in the Black Forest until a little boy named Timothy found it and took it home. This time, I was rescued by a Moon Fairy and my two friends, Michael the leprechaun and Sparkle, the fairy of the Sparkling Silver Stream.'

'You have a friend who is a leprechaun?' I asked.

'Yes, Michael and Sparkle are very good friends. We look after the Green Woodland and the Great Meadow,' he explained.

'Has the darkness ever been lifted from the Black Forest? I mean, have things ever been put right?' I asked.

Chapter Three

The little elf leaned back and said, 'Some time ago, an Ice Crystal found its way into the Sparkling Silver Stream. The Fairy Sea Queen said it came from the heavens, the vastness of space. It changed the Black Forest back in to the Green Woodland and turned the maze back to the Great Meadow. It brought the sparkle back to the Silver Stream and changed the Black Castle back into the little Woodland Cottage. The Black Witch changed back into the grey-haired old lady.'

'Is that the grey-haired old lady I spoke to this morning?' I asked.

'Yes,' answered Tassel. He went on, 'The Ice Crystal separated the Good Magic from the Black. The Fairy Sea Queen locked the Black Magic in a treasure chest and sank it in a very deep rock pool in her caves. Then we watched the Ice Crystal leave the Fairy Sea Queen's caves. It picked up a lot of speed and rose into the air. We watched it until it was gone into space where it had came from.'

'That must have been such a sight,' I said.

'It was,' answered Tassel.

He thought for a moment. I had the impression that he may not tell me what happened next. But after a long silence, he started to speak again.

'When I left the Fairy Sea Queen, she gave me a Magical Golden Belt.'

'Why?' I asked.

'When the Ice Crystal changed things back, it also took our magical powers away. Sparkle was the first to notice, but we had all lost our powers. Michael, Sparkle and me. The Magical Golden Belt was a way to restore them. We are not allowed to give magic to each other, but coming from the belt, the power wasn't coming from us. I restored Michael and Sparkle's powers. As for me, I had the

Magical Golden Belt. It was much stronger than my elfin powers,

and allowed me to do much more than I could as an elf.'

'So all was well,' I said.

'Not really,' said Tassel. He went on, 'The Silver Stream was stolen by the goblins.'

'The whole stream?' I asked.

'From the furthest point of the Green Woodland to the Sea,' said Tassel.

'That must have been a big job!' I said.

'Not really,' answered Tassel.

'The Goblin King had found Michael's crock of gold, and used the first wish to redirect the Sparkling Silver Stream into their caves. The second wish was to make the water from the stream flow through the caves and out into the Great Meadow to turn it into a Marsh.'

Tassel paused for a moment and then said, 'And the Great Wizard himself would sink beneath it. The third wish was to make the water flowing through the caves magical, so the goblins could wish for anything. That was very dangerous for all the fairy folk everywhere. Michael was the one to send the Silver Stream back into the Green Woodland. He took the old crock and used it as a plug. Once the Sparkling Silver Stream was flowing through the Green Woodland again, the old crock started to glow, its golden colour coming back to it. The Magical Golden Belt gave me the speed and strength to grab the Great Wizard from the Marsh, and that made Michael's crock glow even brighter. We had undone two of the wishes, but when the last wish was granted to the Goblin King, Michael was whisked up into the air.'

'Where was he going?' I asked.

'He was going back to Nowhere. That is, the Master Shoemaker's Workshop. A place where the leprechauns learn everything. It would have meant one hundred years there for him. But because of the great magical power in the Magical Golden Belt, I was able to snatch him out of the air just before he entered the Spiral of Spinning Sparkling Stars.'

'Is that the way into the Master Shoemaker's Workshop?' I asked.

Tassel answered with one word. 'Yes,' he said. Then he was silent. When he spoke again, he said, 'I have told you where the crock of gold is. It will be safe there, won't it?'

'Then it's in the goblin caves,' I said.

'Yes,' answered Tassel. 'It is stopping the caves from flooding, and making the Sparkling Silver Stream flow through the Green Woodland.'

'I will not look for it, and I shall not tell of it's whereabouts,' I said. I could tell that what I had said had made Tassel feel more at ease. 'Was everything at peace in the Green Woodland?' I asked.

'No,' answered Tassel. I leaned back on my backpack and I listened to Tassel as he explained about the Treasure Chest of Magic.

Chapter Four

'While standing in a fairy ring in the Great Meadow, the Goblin King made a wish,' said Tassel. 'He wished for a leprechaun, and his wish was granted. Brian appeared from Nowhere. He was dressed in dark green and had very big eyebrows. He was dressed in dark green because he hadn't finished learning about everything yet. The Goblin King told him to bring him the Treasure Chest of Magic. He said he would find it near the sea, and to follow the Sparkling Silver Stream. So Brian started his journey to find the Treasure Chest of Magic.

'Because he was following the Silver Stream, he met Michael and Sparkle, and they brought Brian to me. When they had told me what they had to do, I went with them to the sea. When we reached the sea, Surf was waiting for us. He took us to the Fairy Sea Queen's caves. Surf said he would wait at the caves entrance for us, and Michael, Sparkle, Brian and I went in to see the Fairy Sea Queen. We told her why we had come, and she took us to the rock pool where the Treasure Chest of Magic was. I used my Magical Golden Belt and it enabled me to breathe underwater.'

'You were able to breathe water?' I said.

'Oh, yes,' answered Tassel. 'It's not as nice as air,' he said, and then he went on, 'I touched my Magical Golden Belt and started to turn green. I stepped into the rock pool and began to swim down. I didn't know it was so deep. It was frightening. Then I saw the Treasure Chest of Magic, but I also saw a black and gold monster of the deep.

It frightened me at first, but then it helped me to retrieve the Treasure Chest of Magic. It enclosed me in a bubble and sent me back to the surface of the rock pool. Now we had to let Brian give the Treasure Chest of Magic to the Goblin King, and then take it away from him again. Surf, that is, the Great Wizard, said to give it to the Master Shoemaker. A place where it cannot be opened.'

'Why can it not be opened?' I asked.

'Oh, that's easy,' said Tassel. 'The Fairy Sea Queen has the key, and the Master Shoemaker has the Treasure Chest of Magic, and to enter either place takes a lot of magic.'

'So the Treasure Chest of Magic is safe now,' I said.

'Yes, it is. None of the Black Magic within it will ever be set free in our world or yours,' said Tassel.

Then he continued with his account of how he and Michael delivered the Treasure Chest of Magic to the Master Shoemaker.

'Michael, Sparkle, Brian and I travelled to the goblin caves so that Brian could give the Treasure Chest to the Goblin King. This he did and, as soon as the Goblin King held it, Brian vanished. The wish had been granted. As soon as Brian vanished, I snatched the Treasure Chest from the Goblin King. But when I did, one of the other goblins grabbed Sparkle and locked her in a four-sided black lantern. The goblin shouted, "Give back the Treasure Chest or your stream fairy will spend the rest of her life granting us the wish of light for our caves!"

'I didn't want to leave Sparkle there, but I couldn't let the Goblin King have the Treasure Chest, and so I gave it to Michael. I touched the Magical Golden Belt and asked it for speed and the power to fly. I grabbed Michael by his belt and we left the goblin caves at great speed and took to the sky.

'We arrived very quickly at the Spiral of Spinning Sparkling Stars. This time I allowed Michael and myself to be dragged into it. It was very beautiful as we moved through it. It did make me feel dizzy. Then we entered a white cloud. When it cleared we were in the middle of the Master Shoemaker's Workshop.

'To my surprise, we saw Brian working at one of the many workplaces. When he saw us his eyebrows almost vanished into his hair. The Master Shoemaker soon appeared to us. "I have been expecting you," he told us. Michael gave him the Treasure Chest of Magic, and the Master Shoemaker assured us that it would never be opened. Then Brian asked if he could send us back. He said he could not help anyone to leave, not even us. But then he whispered something in my ear.'

'What did he say?' I asked.

'He said, "I know to get here will have drained all your magic. But you still have the Magical Golden Belt." We thanked him and said goodbye. I touched my Magical Golden Belt and grabbed Michael and we were engulfed in a white cloud. Soon we were flying upwards through the Spiral of Spinning Sparkling Stars. We were almost out when the Magical Golden Belt used up the last of its power. All the magic was gone and we started to fall back into the Spiral of Spinning Sparkling Stars.

'Then suddenly, a big clawed foot grabbed me. I tried to see what it was. Whatever it was, it was holding Michael in its other foot. It was black and gold, and breathing fire. It was a dragon. I knew it was the Great Wizard, but Michael didn't. The black and gold dragon flew through the clear blue sky. I have never felt so safe. We landed here, in the Great Meadow, and the dragon changed its form back to the Great Wizard. Michael asked if he could restore our magic, but he said the magic would be restored in time. Michael thanked him for saving us, and left us to go home and rest.

'As he turned to leave the Great Wizard said, "Michael, when you have rested, I want you to visit the Fairy Sea Queen. She will have something you must bring back here." We watched Michael as he walked across the Great Meadow.'

Chapter Five

'The Great Wizard then explained to me that the Wizards That Be needed to know that I was worthy of having the powers of a wizard. The Great Wizard had offered them to me some time ago. I refused them but, because they had been offered, I still had to prove myself. The Great Wizard gave the dream of the Treasure Chest of Magic to the Goblin King. He knew that he would want it and cause trouble, which he hoped I would stop. As a result, Sparkle was imprisoned in a lantern and Michael and I lost our magical powers.

'When the Great Wizard realised that my Magical Golden Belt was a gift from the Fairy Sea Queen, he asked me to give it to him, and so I did. He wrapped part of his black and gold cloak around it, then he said, "Tassel, this is yours."

'He handed back the Magical Golden Belt. Then he said, "The Wizards That Be say I am not allowed to give you magic, but I can give to you, in all the best legends of fairy folk, three wishes. They are in the three crystals that I have placed in your belt."

'I used the first crystal to give back to Michael his leprechaun magic, and I used the second crystal to free Sparkle, and restore her fairy magic.'

Tassel showed me his Magical Golden Belt and the three crystals. Two were a cloudy blue. The other was sparkling and clear. Then Tassel, the little elf, said something that really surprised me. He took off his Magical Golden Belt and held it out to me.

'Mr. Lawrence, I want you to have this belt. Hold out your hand.'

I did what he asked and he proceeded to tighten the belt around my little finger. When he had finished he said, 'There is one wish left in the last sparkling crystal. You may wish for anything.' He sat down on the grass next to me.

'Anything?' I said. Then I asked, 'Do you know what I will wish for?'

'Yes,' answered the little elf.

I thought for a while, and then, I don't know why, I said, 'I wish that Tassel's elfin magic be restored to him.'

A gentle breeze blew across the meadow. It seemed to say 'The wish is granted'. Tassel looked at me and smiled. 'Thank you, Mr. Lawrence,' he said.

'Did you really know what I would wish for?' I asked.

'Oh, yes,' said the little elf. 'The Great Wizard told me.'

'I didn't know until I said it,' I said.

'Mr. Lawrence, look at the Magical Golden Belt on your finger,' said Tassel

I looked. The last crystal had lost its sparkle and was a cloudy blue, the same as the other two.

'Please keep the golden ring to remind you of me,' Tassel said.

'I will. Thank you, Tassel,' I said.

Just then there was a rustle in the grass, and a moment later a little man dressed in emerald green stepped out and stood next to Tassel. He was carrying a silver belt.

'The Fairy Sea Queen told me to return this to you,' he said.

Tassel thanked him and tightened the silver belt around his waist. Just then, there was another rustle in the grass and a moment later there was another little figure standing next to Tassel.

'Mr. Lawrence,' said Tassel, 'may I introduce you to Michael the leprechaun, and Sparkle, the fairy of the Sparkling Silver Stream.'

'Thank you. I know I am very privileged just to see you,' I said.

Michael was dressed from head to foot in emerald green, except for his brown boots, and the gold buckle on his brown belt. Sparkle, however, was very different. I had never seen a fairy before, but she was something I will never forget. She had long, flowing, golden hair, and a silver band around her forehead. She was wearing a light blue, flowing gown with silver at her shoulders and sleeves. A white belt was at her waist with a silver buckle. Behind her was a very big pair of silver, yet transparent, wings. I just looked at the three little people for some time, totally lost in my surroundings.

Then Tassel said, 'We must leave you now, and thank you for using the last wish. Please be free to tell my stories, we will be quite safe. We can only be found if we want to be found. We can only be seen by those who really want to see us, and we can only be found by those who really want to find us, like those magical places the Great Wizard let you see today.'

I watched the three little people wander into the long grass and then I was all alone in the Great Meadow. It had been a beautiful day and had passed quickly. There was an evening mist falling over the meadow, or the Great Meadow, as I had come to know it. There was a dampness in the air. I took my black and gold cloak from my backpack. Pulling it around my shoulders I started to walk into the chilly, damp mist, in the direction of home. There was just one thought lingering in my mind, 'A wizard can be anything'.

I have never seen Tassel again, although I must confess, I have looked for him. Occasionally the gold ring glows a rich yellow colour, and the three crystals sparkle. Then in a little while the ring just reverts back to the colour of gold, and the crystals become a cloudy blue. I can't help thinking that every time the ring glows like that, Tassel must be having another adventure.

If I ever see him again, I will relate more adventures of Tassel the elf.

9. The Silver Imp

Chapter One

It had been a long warm summer. Now there was a coldness in the air and autumn had arrived. Tassel, the little elf who lived in the little cottage that was close to the Sparkling Silver Stream, had decided to visit his friend the Fairy Sea Queen. She lived in a cave at the far side of the sandy beach that was at the end of the Sparkling Silver Stream.

Tassel untied his little brown boat and set off down stream to the sea. He was dressed in a blue shirt and trousers, with red boots and hat, around his waist he wore a silver belt. He had put a large green cloak into his little brown boat for he knew the evening and night would be cold.

It was quite a long journey but it passed quickly for Tassel. He sailed out of the Green Woodland and it wasn't long before he was pulling his boat out of the water and on to the sandy beach. He left his boat and walked across the beach, at last entering the Fairy Sea Queen's caves.

Tassel didn't know that, as he left the Green Woodland, a strange figure entered it. He appeared at the place were the Sparkling Silver Stream pushes its way between the two large stones and then flows through the Green Woodland down to the sea.

The strange figure was an imp. He was dressed in silver from his head to his feet. A silver hat, silver shirt and trousers, and on his feet he wore silver boots. His name was Bobby Dazzler and, like all imps, he liked to play tricks. He had arrived from Who Knows Where. He didn't know exactly where himself. He just enjoyed being a nuisance.

The Green Woodland seemed to be a very nice place, and so Bobby thought he would stay. He began his new adventure by following the Sparkling Silver Stream. He hopped, jumped and skipped along the grassy bank. Bobby really enjoyed being an imp.

He had long fingers, a pointed nose and pointed ears that folded over at the top. His silver clothes sparkled in the sunlight. They shone so brightly that almost all the fairy folk in the Green Woodland could see him. It was no surprise that Michael the leprechaun, having seen the silver imp shining in the sunlight, went to meet him. Michael waved his hand just above his head and vanished.

He waited until Bobby was close to him, and then he appeared, giving Bobby quite a fright.

'You shine very brightly, don't you,' said Michael. He was standing just in front of the silver imp.

'I do,' came the answer. 'You must be a leprechaun, dressed in emerald green. Don't you find it dull, not being able to shine like me?'

'May I ask you where you are going?' inquired Michael.

'I am following the water,' replied Bobby.

'May I come with you? My name is Michael and you are right, I am a leprechaun.'

'I am always right. My name is Bobby, Bobby Dazzler, and I am an imp. I bet you have never seen anything like me before.'

'I never bet and, no, I have never seen anything like you before,' answered Michael.

The two little people walked side by side along the grassy bank of the Sparkling Silver Stream. Michael was just about to say how pleasant this was when Bobby stuck out his foot and Michael tripped over it. He landed with a bump and rolled down the grassy bank, falling into the Sparkling Silver Stream.

'Oh look,' said Bobby, 'you are all wet.'

'You tripped me,' said Michael.

'Yes I did, didn't I,' he chuckled. 'You did make quite a splash.'

'Well that wasn't a very nice thing to do,' remarked Michael.

'Oh, but I am not very nice,' said Bobby.

'Then I don't think you should go any further into the Green Woodland,' Michael said, as he climbed out of the Sparkling Silver Stream.

Bobby just chuckled to himself. As Michael was just reaching the top of the grassy bank, Bobby gave him just a little push and he tumbled back down the grassy bank, landing with a splash back into the Sparkling Silver Stream, again. When Michael finally climbed out of the water for the second time Bobby was nowhere to be seen. Michael called Bobby two or three times, but there was no reply. Michael thought he should make his way to Sparkle's underwater cave and tell her about Bobby Dazzler, the silver imp.

Michael ran quite quickly through the Green Woodland. When he arrived at Sparkle's Magical Cave the silver imp was all ready there. Bobby was saying something to Sparkle. Michael only overheard the last part of what was said, '...and my magic is much better than yours. Just watch this.'

Bobby, the silver imp, pointed at a tree. 'I can turn it upside down,' he said.

A silver flash flowed from his fingers and the tree's branches lost all their leaves and they turned into roots. The soil from the roots showered down onto Michael and Sparkle. Bobby stepped back so that the soil missed him.

'You can't do things like that!' said Sparkle. She reached out and touched the tree, and its roots turned back into branches, and soon it was covered with leaves again.

'That was good,' said Bobby as he reached into his pocket. He held out his hand to show Michael and Sparkle what he had been reaching for. In his hand there were three little gems. They were transparent and sparkling.

'What are they?' asked Michael.

'They are seeds,' came the reply. 'Watch what happens when I plant them,' said Bobby.

No sooner had he covered the little gems with soil than there was a rumbling in the ground, and then a little brown shoot appeared, and then another two.

'Oh good,' said Bobby. 'All three seeds have taken. You just watch them grow.'

Michael and Sparkle watched as the three little plants grew bigger and bigger. Only a few moments passed and there stood three Gem Trees. Their trunks and branches were gold. They had no leaves, but instead at the end of each branch there was a transparent gem. Around the trunk of each tree the soil was turning purple, and then turned into Amethyst Crystal. Once the three Gem Trees were fully grown, and it didn't take long, they started to drop their transparent gems. Each gem started to grow into a Gem Tree almost as soon as it touched the ground. The purple crystal spread from tree to tree and it wasn't long before the Green Woodland had become the Crystal Forest.

'Can you stop the crystals spreading?' asked Sparkle.

'I don't want to stop the crystals spreading. I think they look very nice,' replied Bobby.

'But nothing can live in a Crystal Forest,' argued Sparkle.

'It doesn't matter to me,' said the silver imp.

'I have something that might stop this in my cave,' Sparkle said as she flew into the air but, just as she dived into the water, Bobby pointed at the Sparkling Silver Stream, there was a silver flash from his fingers and it became Rock Crystal. Sparkle was caught like a butterfly in a piece of Amber Crystal.

'Change the stream back to water,' demanded Michael.

'Oh, I can't do that,' said Bobby. 'That is a job for you,' he chuckled.

Michael didn't know what to try first. He pointed his finger at Sparkle and a green light flowed from his hand.

'Free Sparkle from the stream,' he said, but to his dismay the green light just bounced off the Rock Crystal.

'Your magic isn't as good as mine,' said Bobby. 'Look, I can even make time stand still,' he boasted.

Everything stopped. There was not a sound throughout the Crystal Forest.

Chapter Two

Far away beyond the sky there is a Spiral of Spinning Sparkling Stars. It leads the way to a truly wonderful place called Nowhere. It is the Master Shoemaker's Workshop. A place for fairy folk of all types.

Now that the Green Woodland was in so much danger, the Great Wizard of the Great Meadow sent a message on a Golden Leaf written in black letters, beyond the sky and through the Spiral of

Spinning Sparkling Stars, to arrive in a white cloud in the Master Shoemaker's Workshop. As soon as the white cloud appeared Brian, the little man who longed to be a leprechaun, stood next to it, waiting for it to clear.

When the white cloud had completely cleared, Brian picked up the Golden Leaf and took it to the Master Shoemaker. Brian was dressed in dark green. At his waist was a brown belt with a silver buckle. He longed for the time when his clothes would change to emerald green and he would at last be a leprechaun. Brian had one other feature that made him different from the other fairy folk. He had very large eyebrows that moved up and down whenever he became excited. This was one of those times. He gave the Golden Leaf to the Master Shoemaker, his eyebrows bouncing up and down wildly.

The Master Shoemaker was dressed in a suit of sparkling green with a brown apron and very shiny black shoes with a Golden Buckle on each. He always wore a smile on his face and a monocle over one eye.

He read the message silently and, when he had finished he looked at Brian and said, 'Brian, I have something I would like you to do for me.'

Brian's eyebrows moved up and down faster than they had ever done before.

'Yes sir,' he answered with excitement. 'What would you like me to do?'

The Master Shoemaker explained what was in the message. 'The Green Woodland is in great danger. I want you to go there and find the silver imp.'

The Master Shoemaker removed the Golden Buckles from his very shiny black shoes and gave them to Brian who fastened them to his brown boots.

'The silver imp has great magical powers, but he only seems to annoy other fairy folk with them. He could be very dangerous, but he doesn't seem to know that yet. When an imp gets angry his eyes will glow red. Watch out for this. Try not to be to close to him. Imps usually just like to play tricks, but this time he has changed the Green Woodland into a Crystal Forest.'

The Master Shoemaker leaned close to Brian and whispered in his ear. 'You must trick him into putting my Golden Buckles onto his boots. As soon as they are firmly attached they will bring him to me. When he arrives he will lose all his magical powers and all his tricks will be undone. He will stay with me until I find out where he came from, and then I will send him home.'

It was evening, the end of the day, when a white cloud formed in the Master Shoemaker's Workshop. Brian stood next to it. Then the Master Shoemaker said, 'Brian, you have some magic. You could have a lot more.'

He gave Brian a gentle push, and Brian stepped into the white cloud.

'I won't fail you. I should return tomorrow. Goodnight sir,' he said.

'Goodbye Brian,' came the reply.

The Master Shoemaker knew that if Brian was successful, he may not see him again. Then he whispered something Brian didn't hear. 'My little leprechaun,' he said. The white cloud vanished, and so did Brian.

Chapter Three

After a while Michael could hear voices. He had no idea how long he had been trapped in time, but now he could see and hear again, and what he heard surprised him. It was Brian arguing with Bobby Dazzler, the silver imp. Brian was saying, 'Green is much nicer than silver.'

'Oh no, it isn't,' replied Bobby.'

'You look ridiculous with that silver hat on your stupid head,' remarked Brian.

'I will show you who has a stupid head,' said Bobby.

The silver imp was beginning to lose his temper, and his eyes were beginning to turn red.

'Just look at those ridiculous boots,' Brian said, with a giggle in his voice.

'They shine brighter than your boots,' answered Bobby.

'To make your silver boots better than mine,' said Brian, 'you would need my Golden Buckles.'

'Well I will just take them,' said the silver imp. His eyes were now glowing bright red.

'You could never take them,' replied Brian.

'Yes I could. Just watch me!' shouted Bobby

Michael had heard and seen enough. He stepped between Bobby and Brian.

'No Michael,' said Brian, 'stay away from him, I can stop Bobby Dazzler. He is only an imp. I am nearly a leprechaun.'

'Nearly is what I am concerned about,' said Michael.

Before anyone could do anything the silver imp snatched both Golden Buckles from Brian's boots.

'See it's easy for me,' boasted Bobby.

'You will never make them stick to your silver boots,' said Brian. 'Your magic isn't strong enough.'

'I will stop him sticking them to his boots!' Michael exclaimed.

Brian took a grip on Michael's arm. 'Stay away from him, Michael, Look at his eyes,' said Brian. 'He can't make them stick. I think the Golden Buckles don't like him.'

'They will stick to my silver boots,' exclaimed the silver imp. He muttered something Brian and Michael didn't quite hear or understand.

As the Golden Buckles joined as one to each silver boot the silver imp was whisked up into the sky and beyond.

'Where has he gone?' asked Michael.

'He has a very important appointment with the Master Shoemaker. I just hope he remembers to call him sir,' answered

Brian.

A few moments had passed since the silver imp had been removed from the Crystal Forest.

'How can we undo what the silver imp has done? And how can we free Sparkle?' asked Michael.

'When he loses his magical powers, all should be as it was,' replied Brian.

'But how do you know?' persisted Michael.

'The Master Shoemaker told me,' replied Brian.

'Do you mean he sent you?' exclaimed Michael.

'Yes, he did. He told me to stay away from the imp when his eyes turned red, and he gave me the Golden Buckles to put on the imp's boots. I think he has them back by now,' explained Brian.

Then, quite suddenly, the Rock Crystal that was the Sparkling Silver Stream, changed back to water. A moment or two passed and then Sparkle appeared from the water. She flew in two or three circles and then landed on the soft green grass next to Michael and Brian.

Chapter Four

The three little people watched as the Crystal Forest slowly changed back into the Green Woodland. One by one the Gem Trees slowly turned into woodland trees with lots of green leaves, although there were quite a few brown ones too.

Autumn was taking a hold on the Green Woodland. The purple Amethyst Crystal was slowly changing to brown woodland paths. It wasn't long before the Green Woodland was as it should be again.

'Brian,' said Sparkle. 'It is nice to see you again.'

Then Michael explained how Brian had tricked the silver imp into putting the Master Shoemaker's Golden Buckles on to his own silver boots.

'Where is the silver imp?' asked Sparkle.

'He is with the Master Shoemaker,' answered Brian. 'When he finds out where the silver imp came from he will send him home. I think I should be going home too.'

'The Master Shoemaker will take you back when he is ready, but I don't think it will be for some time, after the way you saved the Green Woodland,' stated Michael.

'Do you think he will let my stay?' Brian asked. His eyebrows had started bouncing up and down with excitement again, for he didn't know what was to happen next.

Michael and Sparkle watched as Brian's clothes slowly started to change to emerald green. The buckle of his brown belt lost its silvery shine and turned to gold.

'You are a leprechaun,' Michael said happily.

Brian looked at his reflection in the Sparkling Silver Stream. 'Yes, I am,' he said in amazement.

'Then you will be staying with us in the Green Woodland,' said Sparkle.

'Can I?' asked Brian.

'Your place is with us now,' Michael said.

A few moments passed and then another wonderful thing happened. A crock of gold appeared right in front of Brian.

'Do you think it's for me?' he asked.

'I think the Master Shoemaker sent it,' answered Michael.

Then the three little people heard a voice they recognised. 'Hello,' it said.

Michael, Sparkle and Brian watched as Tassel tied his little brown boat to some nearby reeds. As he walked towards them he said, 'Brian, its nice to see you again. Are you going to stay this time?'

'He is, this time. Just look at his clothes,' exclaimed Michael.

'Look,' said Sparkle. 'Here is his crock of gold.'

'I will help you to hide that later,' Michael said to Brian.

Tassel sat on the grassy bank with his three friends. 'Did I miss anything while I was visiting the Fairy Sea Queen?' he asked.

Brian spoke first, his eyebrows moving up and down again. 'There was the silver imp,' he said. 'His eyes turned red.'

'You did stay away from him when that happened,' stated Tassel.

'Yes,' said Michael and Brian together.

Michael asked 'Why should we stay away from him, when his eyes turn red?'

'His magical powers would have been at their strongest. He could have done almost anything. He could have been very dangerous,' replied Tassel.

'How do you know about imps?' asked Brian.

'The Great Wizard told me,' answered Tassel. 'How did you know about them?'

'The Master Shoemaker told me,' he said.

They laughed. Then Sparkle spoke, 'The Green Woodland was turned into a Crystal Forest.'

Then Michael spoke, 'Time was made to stand still,' he said.

Then Tassel asked, 'Where is the silver imp now?'

Brian answered, 'He has gone to see the Master Shoemaker. I don't think we will see him again, not at least for one hundred years.'

'It sounds like I missed quite an adventure,' remarked Tassel.

His friends answered together. 'Yes,' they said.

'Everything is as it should be,' stated Michael.

The four friends talked for a long time, happy in each other's company. The Great Meadow, the Green Woodland and the Sparkling Silver Stream right down to the sea, were all safe. Everything was peaceful, throughout this magical place.

The End